Praise for *The Book of Susan*

"In *The Book of Susan*, Hutsell takes the mysteries of the highs and lows of bipolar illness and skillfully intertwines them on the page. Written from the unique perspective of Susan—the one who discovers her diagnosis—it's a page-turner of a story and yet a book to be slowly studied for the genuine wisdom it reveals."
—**Katherine James**, author of *Can You See Anything Now?*
and *A Prayer for Orion*

"Profound and compulsively readable, *The Book of Susan* complexifies typical notions of Appalachia and offers us an unforgettable character in lyrical and accessible prose. Hutsell is a literary stylist who knows how to keep the reader in her grip."
—**Silas House**, author of *Southernmost*

"A riveting first-person account of a woman's realization that she suffers from Bipolar I disorder. Hutsell's protagonist accepts, overcomes, and reinvents her life through her newfound faith, discovered quite by accident due to the disease's delusions. 'God fled me on those days,' she tells us when her illness begins to tear apart her carefully planned life. But Susan emerges transformed, and without sanctimony gives an account of the power of spiritual seeking to pick up the shattered pieces of life. Anyone who encounters a mental disorder in themselves or a loved one will be gripped by this powerful, raw, honest, and intriguing voice."
—**Rita Sims Quillen**, author of *Wayland*

THE
BOOK OF
SUSAN

a novel

MELANIE K. HUTSELL

Raven

PARACLETE PRESS
BREWSTER, MASSACHUSETTS

TO EVERYONE WHO KNOWS WHAT IT IS TO LIVE WITH MENTAL ILLNESS

////// //// //////

2022 First Printing

The Book of Susan, A Novel

Copyright © 2022 by Melanie K. Hutsell

ISBN 978-1-64060-767-5

The Raven name and logo are trademarks of Paraclete Press.

Library of Congress Cataloging-in-Publication Data
Names: Hutsell, Melanie K., 1973- author.
Title: The book of Susan / Melanie K. Hutsell.
Description: Brewster, Massachusetts : Paraclete Press, 2022. | Summary: "A
    spare first-person novel that examines the repercussions of a mental
    illness diagnosis in a modern woman's life"-- Provided by publisher.
Identifiers: LCCN 2021062750 (print) | LCCN 2021062751 (ebook) | ISBN
    9781640607675 (trade paperback) | ISBN 9781640607682 (epub) | ISBN
    9781640607699 (pdf)
Subjects: LCSH: Mentally ill women--Fiction. | LCGFT: Novels.
Classification: LCC PS3608.U868 B66 2022 (print) | LCC PS3608.U868
    (ebook) | DDC 813/.6--dc23/eng/20220103
LC record available at https://lccn.loc.gov/2021062750

10 9 8 7 6 5 4 3 2 1

Published by Paraclete Press
Brewster, Massachusetts
www.paracletepress.com

Printed in the United States of America

TODAY

I wonder where to begin and how.

Though this is actually the end, I suppose. Not of me, but of the book you hold, since what comes next will have already gone before.

To myself, to the countless, nameless others I will never know, who may never have this chance, I have a duty. Some might even say, a call.

I'll start where I am, I guess.
(Can one really begin anywhere else?)

I lived in the mountains of upper East Tennessee in 2005.
As I did as a child. As I do now.
This landscape where I find myself might be unexpected to a visitor. Several small cities—with industry, a college, many libraries—are situated in this river valley.
Edenton, the town with the little public college, has become a tourist's particular and charming surprise, growing fast like all of Boone County, burgeoning with restaurants and boutiques, a diverse population. Home to the area's public radio station.
Millsborough, the stalwart industrial hamlet where I was born, mirrors much of Holston County, mostly white and aging,

shrinking all the time. Like Windy Grove, a proud old railroad town with a skeletal business district. Or the multitude of farming communities that keep on with their dwindling, such as Clemtown, where my father is from and where I grew up, or Blue, the county seat.

It's difficult, I think, to extricate my story from this inheritance. In this part of the world, the rounded, folding, green mountains, among the oldest that exist, are the central reality. You can travel nowhere they are not. You can never not be aware of them.

They hold up the very sky.

Though I still live in the same patch of earth which I've described—where I also resided back in 2005—you cannot measure the distance I have traveled since then in miles or even in light-years.

It is a shift in continents. It is a transfiguration of a lifetime.

I
SUSAN

(FIRST SUSAN)

I couldn't imagine how it could be difficult. That morning I had energy, and I had optimism, and the day began resplendent with sun, and the evening was set to turn lush and hot, the perfect night for our party.

All misgivings were erased from my mind as if they'd never been.

Except, of course, for Lorraine.

Samuel stood by the kitchen sink with a glass of orange juice in his hand and watched me as I packed Ian's lunch. "You're sure you're up to this?"

"Yes, Samuel, we've been over it, what is there for me to do?"

"That was the idea. But I want you to tell me if we need to call this off."

I finished my coffee, set the mug in the dishwasher. "No, I feel fine, better than fine, actually. If I can't manage this, then there's no hope for me. You and Jim are going to grill the meat, so all I need to do is get it in the marinade when I get home." I meant to shop that day. A number of purchases, items endlessly essential, it now seemed so clear—new dress and shoes and necklace to match, the religious study book with the title that had spoken straight to me—a whirl of plans to combat her schemes. I zipped the soft-side lunch bag. "Meredith's going to help me set up the patio, and then the catered stuff comes, and then you'll come, and everything should all turn out."

"I would like to suppose there's hope for you," said Samuel.

I felt the dark ripple through my morning.

"I'm trying," was all I could say, "but no one calls me back." Not even the secretary, I'd noticed.

"Maybe you should try somewhere else."

That was what I was starting to think, but I couldn't believe it, I just couldn't. God wouldn't ignore me that way. "I don't want to give up yet." I ran some more water in the vase of orange and yellow daylilies, cut that morning. Put it back on the counter.

"Giving up would not be like you," he said. "And I don't recall that that was what was said."

"Okay, yes, I understand," I said. "Let me think about it. I've got to get Ian. We need to get on the road."

"I'll see you tonight," he said, as I turned to leave the room. "Be careful with yourselves."

Ian sat in his highchair eating the last of his dry Cheerios with that stuffed sheep, Lammykin, snug and eyeing me in the crook of his arm. It was still hard for me to face my son. But today I felt that being a good mother could begin again, that I could come to understand why I'd stopped.

Perhaps God would reveal that to me, too, in the book I'd been given to write.

"Mommy go?" said Ian, his mouth full. He thrust Lammykin and his empty bowl toward me.

The door closed as Samuel began his weekday morning trip to the courthouse.

"Come on," I said, walking to retrieve my son from his highchair—much more patiently on this absurdly beautiful Friday in June—"let's go get this day."

///// //// ///// // ////////

So here's how Lorraine became a reality to my life.

We were at breakfast, Samuel, Ian, and I. Eating hard-boiled eggs and English muffins. The last of the baby-pink Valentine's roses from Samuel slowly, faintly withering, as our table's centerpiece. Extra-crisp bacon set out for Samuel and Ian, slices of orange for Ian and me.

"Mike Davis's wife," Samuel said, "would enjoy joining us on Tuesdays."

Ever since it had begun, three years before, our Tuesday circle had continued unchanged.

"He mentioned she's a banjo player looking for some friends to make a little music with," said Samuel, "so I mentioned our little soiree. I didn't see the harm."

I have always been more territorial than I would like to admit. "Of course not. It'd be good for her."

"It would be a kindness. Mike's certainly been an outsized help to me in the time he's worked here."

I assumed Mrs. Davis and her husband, Samuel's new judicial secretary, were good country people, since that's how Samuel had said they came to us in Millsborough, each from some humble household somewhere. No sin in any case, but after my childhood days in Clemtown, I'd purposely escaped proximity to rural ladies and good old boys with their starched consciousnesses and grave-narrow interests. I wondered how unfettered our Tuesday evenings could remain with the *perhaps* of Mrs. Davis's conservative sensibilities among us.

But I also reminded myself that was not the consideration most charitable to give.

"I think it's a lovely idea." Wet washcloth at the ready, I wiped the honey sticky and crumbs from Ian's mouth and hands. "Please tell her she should come and bring her banjo."

"Consider it done," Samuel said.

I did.

Tuesday came, and everyone was there. Nell with her fiddle, Jim with his bodhrán. Charles had two new poems. Old Sarah carried a news clipping that tallied the dead in Iraq and her red tambourine. With a small bowl of animal crackers and Goldfish, Ian bunkered with his stuffed giraffe near the fireplace, but not too near, under Meredith's supervision. Meredith had helped me with the canapés, and there was red and white wine, all on the coffee table, while coffee itself was in the kitchen, spreading its deep, woodsy smell to every downstairs room. I'd carried down my dulcimer, and Samuel presided as himself from his homely, well-worn, slate-gray recliner.

When the doorbell rang, I was the one to answer.

"Hi." The young woman on the front porch had her instrument case over her shoulder. "Are you Mrs. Ellison?" She was neither tall nor short nor very remarkable-looking, but she had dark eyes that were bright and lively, as though they were seldom still.

I wanted to correct her—*I'm Dr. Huffman*—but decided against saying anything that sounded so cold. I smiled. "Please, call me Susan."

She thrust out her hand as though she was some gee-whillikers, pre-pubescent lad of another era. "Lorraine Davis. Pleased to meet you." Her hair was tousled, her smile was good-natured, and she was pink-cheeked like a dairymaid.

I reached and pressed her hand. "We're so glad to have you join us tonight. Come right in." Lorraine Davis had a warm, fervent hand.

She shed her coat in the foyer and followed me to the living room. Sarah, Jim, and Charles called out welcome.

Nell nodded and said hello. (I'd confided some of my misgivings to Nell, days before.)

Ian watched from his play spot.

Samuel stood. "Well, it appears you found us all right."

I loved how Samuel could use his imposing size and mighty voice to set a person at ease.

"Yes, thank you. Thank you all very much." Lorraine had seen Ian. "Why, hello there!"

She stepped toward him. In her eagerness, at least, she seemed not much older than Ian, but I knew that Lorraine and I couldn't be far apart in age.

Ian clapped his hands over his eyes.

"What's your name, cutie pie?" Lorraine brought her face close to his.

Ian peeked at her from between his fingers.

"You know what, you can help me," she said. "I bet you know everyone's names. Can you tell me their names?"

He shook his head no. Then he grinned and pumped his head up and down for yes. My sweet baby, who had come to us at a most inconvenient time, and yet I had no sorrow about that choice and wanted no pity. Not all of my colleagues understood this. I don't know if I understood it.

"Who is that?" Lorraine pointed to Samuel.

"Daddy." Ian looked at Samuel rather than at Lorraine. Hands away from his face now, he twisted his fingers together, tugged them, scrunched them. "That Daddy."

"Who's she?"

"Mommy." The directness of Ian's look as he looked at me, the certainty in his voice, rendered me abject and weak and also swelled me with the sweetness of knowing what we shared—a belonging just for the two of us, forever.

Lorraine pointed to each person in the room, asking my son's assistance, and Ian, with some assistance himself, named them all.

Even I was charmed by Lorraine's openness. Inundated, but intrigued. Perhaps she and I were escapees alike. Perhaps the dread of long, desolate driveways had brought her to that very room, to that very hour, as it had brought me. I felt stained.

"Now," Lorraine said. "Who's this?" She tapped Ian's shoulder.

"Me Ian!"

"And do you know who I am?"

He snorted and covered his face again. "Sweetie girl."

The general rise of laughter lifted everything around me. It lifted everything in me. Lorraine's smile was wide and girlish and invited conspiracy. When she moved, she was the brightest thing in sight. I could never object to her being among us. That had been petty and paltry, utterly base of me. It would be splendid to have her in our circle.

The surfaces of the room glowed.

In that moment, I don't know that I was in the least disturbed. But I have never been sure.

///// //// ///// // ///////

*B*efore Lorraine's arrival, and before the onset of the other, my life prospects had looked like this:

In my mentor's office, one wall was dedicated to women in academia. Black-and-white photos showcased academic pioneers from the earliest coed days at our college. In color pictures, women gave lectures, commencement addresses. Women posed in groups at conferences. Women shook hands with Dr. Evelyn Rickwell.

Dr. Rickwell began our meeting—in January of 2005—by asking about Ian.

I couldn't help but hand my wallet across the desk to show his picture, though I recognized this might not be the best way to begin. "He's almost two and a half."

"Oh!" She smiled. "Precious. Hard to believe he's getting so big." She handed back the wallet. "Is the chancellor well?"

She did not mean our college chancellor. She meant my husband, the chancery court judge.

"Yes," I said, stowing the wallet in my bag again.

Dr. Rickwell did not, as a rule, ask about Samuel. I'd always assumed this was because she felt, consciously or not, that he was a topic to be avoided in discussions surrounding my progress toward tenure. Even on that day, she did not say his name. As if, by keeping him nameless, she could keep him unmentioned, too.

However, I never took offense. If her omission was her means of letting my work stand on its own merits, then I was grateful of the opportunity.

When I was newly arrived in Edenton, in the fall of 2001—in East Tennessee once more, but returned as a history professor, and single still—I had first asked about the photographs on Dr. Rickwell's wall. She'd told me, "They're here because they're my she-roes." A petite Black woman with a commanding presence in any space she occupied, she'd swept her hand in their direction. "I put them on my wall," she said, "to inspire me. To remind me of the indomitable ones who made it possible for me to be here. And to honor the brave ones who work alongside me. It's an important work we do in this place, and I should not forget that and never take it for granted."

As I had surveyed those photographs of *the brave ones*, I resolved was going to make my way onto Dr. Rickwell's wall someday.

"So? Susan?" she said to me now, "I think you're looking good. It's all here. Your record of scholarship, the teaching award your first year and continued praises of your teaching ability. Fall semester, 2002, of course, you didn't teach, but you produced work that led to publications later, even as you negotiated your new role and responsibilities as a mother. I understand you're working with Dr. Mackey and others on a symposium for this fall?"

"Yes, that's right." The chance to work with Hugh on a project that would spotlight German immigrant influences in the Appalachia of East Tennessee and enhance my curriculum vitae as well was too fantastic to pass up.

Dr. Rickwell leaned forward from the other side of her desk. "You've had a full life since coming here but stayed dedicated to your work. I see no reason why you won't be an excellent candidate when you start the process of going up for tenure in the fall."

I restrained my smile. My heart felt like it would arrow into the sky.

I never really knew how often my colleagues perceived and treated me as Mrs. Ellison rather than as Dr. Huffman. I suspected it happened rather less than I feared, but more than I believed.

In Dr. Rickwell's office, though, I never doubted where I stood—I was respected as a woman who lived by her mind. Before my career was over, I intended everyone to know what I could accomplish with it.

///// //// ///// // ///////

*[T*o illuminate things still more—
here is how Samuel used to tell
the district attorney
the mayor and assorted dignitaries of Millsborough
fellow jurists at the courthouse in Blue
the director of the museum and the conductor of the
symphony orchestra
the members of our merry band as well as their companions
who floated through the gatherings at our house
and all those who wanted to hear—and likely some who
didn't—
the story of our meeting:

I was waiting for someone else entirely, who hadn't bothered to call and was fifteen minutes late. I was standing outside Benedict's, in Edenton. It was October and nearly dark, getting colder by the minute and starting to rain, of course. Just then Shirley called to say she wasn't going to be able to make it—having more trouble with her mother—she was sorry. A shame and an unfortunate situation. I told her not to worry, and she said the same and to go on without her.

She and I hadn't been out together but only the once before, you understand. Shirley's a fine woman, she really is, but I suppose it wasn't our time.

That October was unnerving, though, I will say, so soon after 9-11. You remember how confounded and strange. Time to reconsider security at the courthouse, the chemical plant. To rethink a lot of things.

*So there I was, hanging up my phone and managing to get it
into my coat pocket while keeping the rain off with the umbrella,
trying to decide if it was still the night for dinner and Britten, when
here comes this tall, blonde woman along the sidewalk under an
umbrella of her own. She's got something tucked under her arm,
a book maybe, and she's coming nearer, and I can see she's young,
late twenties, but with a thoughtful expression. A sophisticated
look about her. Even in that God-awful weather, her hair's like a
cloud. All those curls, the color of honey.*

To Samuel's account, I usually interjected here that if you got
to moisturize and detangle my hair, you would not find it very
cloudlike.

Beyond that, I never knew how to respond to this description of
myself. Who am I to say what he saw? I can only speak from my
own vantage point: earlier that day, I'd emerged from my apartment
to do solo lunch and a little downtown window shopping—assaying
something like normal after the terror of September—and so was
dressed up more than I might have been, and was headed home
from the bookstore. I had, incidentally, purchased the umbrella on
the way out of the store. I was coming upon a distinguished-looking
older gentleman standing outside a fine dining establishment, the
sort of restaurant where financially secure and cultured people
would mingle. He looked a little lost, like he might have received
disheartening news. He also looked like the kind of man who might
smoke a pipe in a deep armchair in the evenings in his study. This
observation caused me to linger a little in my observing, since I
have always been taken by the idea of a man like that.

Though, in fact, I am no great lover of smoking.

The story, as Samuel told it, goes on from here:

So I said to myself, what the hell, it's a miserable enough evening already, and I move to intercept her. She stops, and I don't think she looks much surprised.

"Good evening, ma'am," I say, "have you ever seen Britten's opera A Midsummer Night's Dream?*"*

She says no, but she recalls the Shakespeare play as a "delightful romp about love and a donkey." So I say, "Well, I'm Chancellor Ellison, and I find myself in Edenton this evening with two tickets and only one attendee. If you find yourself free, and would be gracious enough to accept my invitation, you would be entirely welcome to attend both dinner and the opera with me."

As I remember it, Samuel did not announce to me that he was *Chancellor Ellison*, just like that, since that isn't at all a thing he would do. I believe this detail of his is storytelling shorthand, and that in fact he would have introduced himself as Samuel Ellison and explained to me later who that was.

But the distinction between our versions of our first encounter is probably irrelevant. The result was probably the same. I suppose it was.

The part of the story I can't really supply, though, that really is mysterious to me in every way, is why, alone on a darkening sidewalk in the rain, accosted by a complete stranger bent on offering a date to another complete stranger, I opened my mouth and answered *yes*.

It was a fortunate thing to say. It was not the wrong thing.)

////// //// ////// // ///////

After Lorraine's first visit to our home—interestingly enough—in February of 2005, on the following Sunday, I encountered another, altogether different guest. And with that, a very different sort of beginning.

I had no way to know what was happening to me, what to expect. There is no way to expect a heavenly visitation.

Samuel had gone to church—the correct place, he felt, for a chancellor to be on a Sunday in East Tennessee—and had taken Ian, and I was alone in the house. I sat at my desk in my study in the sun of late winter with a sturdy mug of black coffee and a cup of strawberry-banana Yoplait nearby. I was writing a call for submissions for the fall symposium. My sock feet were in the chair with me, my knees mountained against the desk, so that the computer screen seemed far away.

I cradled the mug of coffee in both hands. The quiet of the house weighed more than I'd first thought. I considered putting on some music.

Around me, the room removed, grayed into shadow.

(At the time, of course, I barely noticed. I'm reaching as I think back to that day, grappling with how to articulate what came over me.)

In the same breath, I was expanded, my chest poured full of warmth and light. My ears tingled.

Splendor arose in that feeling of expanse, a vast surge of goodwill.

My eyes looked on a space above me.

Saturated with blue.

There was and was not a table there.

I mean that I could see it, only not like I saw the bookshelves, my desk.

Like it came into my mind so plainly that it was right there before me.

With a pale cross above it, as though suspended on an unseen wall.

My heart kicked upwards and kept right on. I kept on breathing, too.

A voice electrified the flesh of my neck and sizzled along my arms.

You could declare new ways.

It did not utter itself in the air but stamped across my mind, resonated in my ears, emphatic, specific, like nothing I could have summoned.

The fear arrived then, because the moment had gone. I was alone in a body, in a place turned strange to me, and I had no earthly way to understand.

My palms permeated by the good, steaming liquid in the mug.

The patient, pulsing cursor. Awaiting any keystroke.

I would have thought I was crazy, except I knew Mamaw's story. God came to her one Sunday morning when she was a girl, and she'd gone on to raise chickens and children and grandchildren—one grandchild, anyway—to churn butter and to knead biscuit dough. At seventy-four, she'd killed a snake in her garden with a hoe. There wasn't anything crazy about her.

I took a drink of coffee. My hands did not shake.

I was also intimately familiar with the life of Anna Maria Magdalena Muller, the subject of my dissertation, my primary research focus. I couldn't say if the visions she'd recorded in her journal in early nineteenth-century East Tennessee were true, were real, but they'd certainly altered her life and impacted the lives of many people, especially the women, in her community.

As for me and what I'd come to believe, I knew enough biblical textual scholarship to convince me forever that the words in that book were authored by human beings, like the words of all literary works. And the universe seemed miraculous enough to me without the existence of God to explain it. The most staggering chance out of all the chances that could be was that, out of nothing and nowhere, our reality emerged, and yet, here it was, all around us, very real, every day.

I lowered my knees, set down the mug. I did not glance up to see the place where the vision was not.

It had burrowed deep, somehow, tucked snug behind my ribs.

Until I could puzzle out what had happened, think it through, learn more, and say for certain what this occurrence had meant, I would say nothing about it to anyone. It felt right to hold it close and also to hold it in abeyance. I wanted to keep what I had seen for myself. That was my resolve.

I scooted my chair closer and leaned into the work.

////// //// ////// // ///////

Mamaw met God when she was ten years old. She told me she was sitting by her sister in the pew one Sunday morning, and the preacher was saying words as he would have done any Sunday, when without any willing of her own, any thought more strange arising than the various thoughts of numberless other mornings, there entered into her a presence that was wholly other than herself. It brought a clarity like a field in winter, the ground white and clean, the trees edging it stripped of all but their very selves, naked to the sky.

She didn't use those words to describe what happened.

I *was a-sittin there,* she said, or something rather like it, *and before I knowed, Jesus had come into my heart, and I was saved that very minute. Oh, I knowed I was, and I was just so glad, and I begun a-cryin, too. I could see Jesus knowed me, his eyes see every little thing, and yet he loved me more than all, just how it said in the Bible, and he loved everybody like he loved me, there wasn't no difference.*

At the time this happened to her, Mamaw had never laid eyes on Hulda Huffman, the woman I later knew. She had no notion that such a person might ever exist. She was someone else—the girl, Hulda Bishop—a girl who had to have been alive once, I know, but only in a world where the now-certainty of all that came after—including me—was not certain at all, was in fact the merest slip of a chance.

That world of hers appears to me only in fragments—in photographs, books, and movies. I've accumulated a reasonable heap of them. But even with my sense of historicity, with my shadows of knowledge, I can't really know those times. My mind still can hardly stretch wide enough to fit Hulda Bishop in.

Yet most of my life I've carried inside me the sight of a girl dressed in white standing in the water of the creek running by that church in Clemtown. The light of that day is pale, the trees are leafy green, the small congregation is clumped along the creek bank. I can hear the relentless water over everything. The preacher tips the girl back. It covers her in that hovering moment that is swift and brief and lasts a lifetime. Then she streams back up out of it. The water running off her, soaking into her, and I experience the certainty of Mamaw's experience.

When she told me the story of how God entered her life, her words engendered in me this little touchstone instant. I keep it because it mattered to Mamaw and because it has become a truth to me, an emblem of dignity and possibility, a knowledge of the way things can be in the world.

But this scene that I treasure must be fabricated at least in part. Mamaw never described any white clothing or the cast of the light on the morning she was baptized, so I, too, must be present in this remembrance.

And I suppose that is unavoidable and also necessary. How can I have this memory if no facet of it was ever mine?

////// //// ////// // ////////

After much thought—in the days following the vision—I finally decided I was not about to go with Samuel and Ian to the church they attended most weeks, and where occasionally I joined them, such as on Christmas Eve and Easter.

If I went with them, Samuel would be able to see in my face why I was there. Of course he would. He knew me too well.

I drove in a different direction altogether.

The road was the road, and the sky was the sky, and yet they seemed to exist on an otherworldly plane, or perhaps that was me. Buildings scudded by. The hum and drone and whoosh of passing cars settled over the silence where I sat. The world outside seemed to retreat from me, but it also seemed that the world sat in my chest, beamed through my mind. The effect was revelatory to me.

My hands held the wheel. I was sure of that.

I guided the car into a parking lot at a large church that looked like a warehouse. I had picked this one because I had seen it a few times, driving past, and because I figured no one would notice one more person lurking in the back of the room.

Oh, the day was cold. Oh, I walked through a shivering place, and yet there was going to be warmth for me where I was going. So I hoped.

Here is what I experienced in that building on that day:

Knots of people talking, laughing. Some wearing suits and dresses, some in sweatshirts and blue jeans.

Backs turned to me.

Tables spread with coffee, orange juice, doughnuts from Krispy Kreme.

Myself, threading among the knots of people. Hunched. Coffeeless. Doughnutless. Grateful for all the backs and shoulders.

Pale wintry light descending through windows.

Myself, down a hall and inside an enormous room, like a gym, but the walls black, floor dark, lights dim, with a stage at the front. The backs of more people.

Everything foreign to me in that room. No cross, no baptistery, no American flag, no Bible lying open on no wooden table inscribed, *This do in remembrance of me.*

(But, truthfully, everything foreign to me in the sanctuary of my remembrance, also.)

Rows of padded chairs crammed against one another. I chose a chair on the aisle. Shoved my purse under it, draped my coat over the chair's back.

I sat as far to the rear as it was possible to sit in that room.

My body without joints or blood. My body impermeable. Non-circulatory.

Murmurs and melodies of conversations around me.

My body like desiccated wood.

Myself, waiting in the dark.

Until the room darkened more.

And the lights on the stage intensified.

A wild burst of terror thrummed through me.

Perhaps I would meet God in this room.

Perhaps there was no God to meet.

A clean-cut rock band came out onto the stage. There were microphone stands, a drum set. People clapped and cheered. Everyone around me stood.

With fear and misgiving, I stood, too.

The room exploded in sound—electric guitars, drums and cymbals, human voices. Eyes around me closed. Opened hands drifted about in the air. The glimpses of faces I saw were both quietened and very much alive.

I thought, *They all looked regular enough in the room with the doughnuts and the orange juice.*

Songs' words were projected onto giant screens at the front of the room, but I didn't know the tunes. These weren't "Victory in Jesus," "Love Lifted Me," or any of the songs familiar from the hymnbook in Mamaw's church. It was a chant-like singing with a huge, bone-marrow-deep pulse in the music.

I stood there and tried to feel something. I tried to feel absolutely nothing at all.

If these regular people around me could feel enraptured, could act this way, then what had happened to me maybe could fit into my conceptions of real life. Visions might enter our studies and living rooms all the time, as a matter of course. To those of us alive now, as they did to Mamaw, to Anna Maria Magdalena Muller. Maybe God showed up more often than I thought.

The songs kept coming.

After awhile, I noticed the back of this man's head. The head belonged to a stranger, but I found myself arrested by the vulnerability of the man's ears.

They were shadows. They were uncovered. They were a sight of him he remained entirely unaware of as I took in that sight.

His hair was cropped close against his neck. His neck was a shadow, a fragile spinal column inside a covering of skin.

A sharp shiver like ice cracked loose inside me. It slowly started trickling away. I felt tender toward this man in that moment. I was in the presence of a great and beautiful mystery.

When the music I heard merged with the mystery, I was overpowered. I was completely undone.

I shut my eyes and began to cry.

You could declare new ways. I heard this down to the soles of my feet.

I felt honored. I felt special.

I felt infused with a gigantic love that turned the room on and radiated into everyone and everything in it. The love had no end.

I realized I had to do *something*. I would do anything.

///// //// ////// // ////////

Anna Maria Magdalena Muller, in 1797, moved with her older brother, William, from the home of their father in Wytheville, Virginia, to a new home in the vicinity of what is now Windy Grove, Tennessee. She was seventeen at the time. William's wife, Catherine, journeyed with them.

Anna Maria kept a diary, partly in German, partly in English, from 1803 to 1810 that chronicled her religious experiences. Raised Lutheran, influenced by Methodism in her new East Tennessee community, she recorded seven visions she claimed to have received in 1803, over the course of nine months while leading a weekly women's devotional group in her brother's home. These revelations, as she called them, convinced her that she was not supposed to marry but should remain entirely free to do God's work. She would devote the whole of her life to prayer and good works.

She cut her hair and, in a time when everyone worked hard, was noted (in recollections taken down long after the fact) for her especial willingness to help the women of neighboring farms with cheerfulness and great patience. She also exhorted young women in the community to follow her example and remain unmarried.

After public characterizations of her behavior as unchristian and numerous acts of vandalism committed by anonymous neighbors against the family, including the slaughter of Catherine's prize hen, Anna Maria was housed in a separate cabin on her brother's farm in 1807. Despite this, many women still sought her out for assistance and for counsel.

The true extent of her influence will never be known, but there are some facts that tantalize. It is known, for example, that one of the neighbor women who had dealings with Anna Maria also had a young daughter who went on, many years later, to marry a Tennessee state politician who supported improved educational opportunities for women. One can only speculate if the grown daughter may have swayed her husband at all in his political stance.

Anna Maria continued to chronicle her life and articulate her beliefs in her diary. She wrote down three more revelations in 1809 that she believed showed her life's work was coming to a close. In 1812, she died of a fever and was buried on her brother's property.

When I went away to college and then to graduate school, I learned what it meant to be from East Tennessee. One classmate asked if I was wearing my first pair of shoes. Another wanted to know if I was afraid to live in the part of the country where I was born and raised. As badly as I wanted to leave Clemtown, as deeply as I never wished to return, I found that I couldn't escape it, that it had followed me in ways I wouldn't have believed. It had burrowed in my flesh. It flavored how I spoke and how others heard me when I did. It made me want to represent my people well. It made me determined to defend my homeland against all comers.

Slowly I realized what I was looking for. There had to be a way to be from East Tennessee that didn't fester in the blood. There had to be a way to redeem my childhood.

I was going to learn and learn and learn. I was going to carry my knowledge back to my people. Through research and teaching, I could help other would-be-escapees like me.

When I discovered Anna Maria, I discovered a woman who had lived in my part of the world and had found a way, despite the strictures of her time, to transcend the circumstances of her life. I found her rooted, self-contained, unashamed. Hers was a quiet but meaningful existence.

Introduced to the first traces of her story, I'd recognized my life's work.

////// //// ////// // ///////

"Hey there, Susan." Hugh's smile always expressed a tender fragility to my mind.

Waylaid as I walked to the circulation desk at the college library, I clutched the books tighter to hide their titles, repositioned my arm so their spines were obscured.

"Ready for all those proposals to come rolling in?" Hugh asked me.

I prayed I wore nothing, carried nothing, possessed no look in my eye that might betray the recent visitation in my study. "Not a bit. In fact, I plan to slack and let them slide as long as possible."

His wobbly laugh punctured my single-mindedness. "Very good! I ought to follow your lead, I suppose? Delete the submissions I receive? Dump them on some unsuspecting T.A.?"

My face fit better now. "Dr. Mackey, you should, of course, never settle for being a pale imitation of me—you should instead pursue that line of inquiry with your own original genius."

"Even better—you stole my part!" Hugh laughed again. He wrinkled the bridge of his nose the way he did now and then to situate his glasses where they belonged. "Because original genius, or discourse on the subject, anyway, I'd say resides more fittingly in the English department than in yours. Though, in my case, it's not so much my area of expertise."

"Mine either, I'm afraid." I hoped I was deflecting attention from the books in my possession. The thoughts I'd been having, the intense feelings about what I'd experienced of God were so very powerful and private that it embarrassed me to stand this close to my colleague and risk his knowledge of them. "But, yes," I went on, "I'll be spending spring break playing blocks and enforcing naptime and devouring proposals. I'll e-mail you when classes reconvene, and we can set a time to meet."

"Excellent! I'll look for your e-mail, and meanwhile, you have a wonderful break, Susan."

"You, too, Hugh."

When Hugh and I had arrived at the college, both of us in the fall of 2001, we'd discovered we had focused on Appalachian studies in our respective fields. That had been pleasant to know in the early days of aloneness in Edenton.

Perhaps I now feared Hugh's scorn, his concern.

He headed for the stacks, and I proceeded to the circulation desk.

But my apprehension was absurd. My thoughts weren't that loud.

Besides, it was natural for me to investigate biblical references in the journal of Anna Maria Magdalena Muller.

That wasn't what I meant to investigate, of course.

///// //// ///// // ////////

I went back to the church. It was early spring, a warmer day.

I saw the clusters of backs. Tables of doughnuts. Shining smears of faces.

I avoided them all.

On the intervening Sunday, I'd worked in the morning in socks and pajamas in my study in an ordinary house. The heat shuddered off and on. The keyboard rattled beneath my fingertips. I ate my toasted English muffin with peanut butter and my blueberry Yoplait. I drank my coffee.

All was very usual. There were no crosses. No voices.

I did notice, however, the slight tremble of thought—a flicker of flame in a draft—inclining toward the row of chairs where I'd hidden in the dark the week before.

I felt once more the overflow of connectedness that had surged into me there.

During the week, at odd times, I would suddenly love everyone around me, whether I knew them or not. My knees buckled, and my eyes brimmed, in those moments when I was overcome by the sheer frailty of human creatures. By their extreme preciousness.

I believed this was what everyone who'd met God came to experience.

I didn't see more visions, but in the pharmacy, I did catch sight of a woman's magazine that touted a relationship quiz inside—*How to Tell if He's for Real.*

To me, the words seemed not a coincidence but a message. They seemed like the question on my mind.

The day that I returned to the church, the car was driving itself.

It was like I was sleeping. It was like I had not climbed in.

I went back to the room with the darkened chairs and the electrified stage.

It's an extraordinary thing, really, how memory doesn't work. I'm sure the church's preacher got up and said things the first time I was there, but I can't recall any impression I had.

Or maybe it was a different preacher—a visiting minister, the youth minister—who spoke that time.

But on this visit I noticed the church's preacher was not the big, jowly, red-faced shouter I expected. He was a young man, short and slight, with an expression of concentration and heedfulness. He spoke from notes or prepared remarks, and his voice was gentle.

You had to listen to hear him. He was a new experience for me.

I don't remember the specifics of his sermon now, but I do remember its substance. He talked about taking care of the less fortunate. Challenged people to see past their own difficult situations and have mercy on others struggling.

He talked about seeing God in those people I find it difficult to like.

What he said arrested me. I'd always thought of church as being a series of exhortations to believe the impossible. I had never thought of it like this man did, as a place to get real about real life.

As I listened, I believed I had to affirm that what was happening to me could happen. That what did not appear to make sense was within the realm of possibility in an ordinary human life like mine.

People could meet God, be confronted by God.

People with doctoral degrees in history. Even people who were not sure of God's existence.

Among a tribe of people whose names I didn't know—but God apparently did—I felt something move in me—in my mind, in my soul—a great, deep welling of certainty and gratitude. I was in a place where I belonged, where I was welcomed, where God was glad to see me.

Driving away from the church, I rolled down the window. I yelled with happiness. I thrust out my arm, opened the fingers of my hand to let the air stream through. On the stereo, I had Emmylou on full blast, and I sang along, all the way home.

///// //// ///// // ///////

So God had become real to me—I was enraptured by what I'd discovered—and that reality overflowed into my every waking moment.

The Bible I used as a research aid came out of my study and took up residence on my nightstand. I bought Bible study books so I could learn more from the experts.

I was a professional scholar, after all. It made sense to me to find out all I could.

To keep my Sunday morning experiences close to me throughout my week, I bought a Christian rock CD for my car. In my rear-view mirror, I spied Ian dancing his giraffe back and forth whenever I played it. His response was the perfect expression of my own happiness.

In accordance with the sermons I heard, I tried harder to bear with people I found hard to bear. When Lorraine exclaimed over the details of her life and everyone else's, irritating me with her extravagance of openness, I responded by offering her more of the crab dip she'd professed such a fondness for, reminding myself I was giving kindness to a newcomer.

If Samuel was bemused by the changes I made, he was tactful enough not to show it. He asked me one thing only, in one of his non-questions on a rare weeknight when we happened to arrive at our bedroom at concurrent times.

He was sitting in the bed, reading. I was emerging from the bathroom and switching off the bathroom light. His nightstand lamp was on.

"I don't understand," he said, looking at his book, "why you won't come with us on Sunday mornings."

I moved toward my side of the bed. I didn't point out that he and Ian could just as easily come with me, because I didn't want them to. And that didn't feel strange to me or bother me in the least, it felt simply so. This was a way I had to go on my own.

"I don't know either, Samuel, I can't explain. But this is something I have to do. For myself."

"Well, far be it from me to interfere with one's exercise of freedom of religion." The archness left his eyes and voice as he looked at me. His face settled as he continued. "Especially if it's something you desire very much."

I nodded, in my nightgown and socks, my face washed and makeupless. "I do."

"Well," he said again. "Then that's how it will be."

I considered his sensible face, that certitude in his voice I'd come to understand. What Samuel gave wasn't the granting of permission, which I would have abhorred, but his statement of—and acceptance of—the truth. I understood the difference, and I loved him for respecting that difference, too, among all the reasons I did love him. I slid under the covers.

"I'll give you anything in my power to give," he said, looking at me still.

"That's not something I have any questions about."

"Good."

We turned out the lights.

///// //// ///// // ////////

Samuel's first wife, Helen, died seven years before our marriage. Samuel's son, Joel—about five, six years younger than I was— lived away at school and then just lived away.

The house where Samuel and I made our home together brimmed with emptiness and echoes when I first stepped into it. It was like nothing so much as a downstairs filing cabinet crammed with yellowed sheaves of papers in yellowed folders. It was tidy and quiet and mostly forgotten, even when you looked right at it. Samuel lived there among the tombs. He kept his eyes set ahead and everything in good order.

Samuel had cooked breakfasts for himself on the weekends. They were not bad breakfasts. His suppers he brought to the house from a favorite restaurant. He hired a cleaning service to take care of the house's inside, but he mowed the lawn and trimmed the hedges himself. When he was not reading for his work, he read biographies and books of history in the evenings or on the weekends. Occasionally he attended the opera.

After our marriage, we worked in separate studies and read together in the living room. We kept the cleaning service, but I didn't mind cooking now and then, honey chicken and broccoli, eggplant parmesan. We went to the opera together and the theatre and the symphony orchestra.

And I invited Edenton friends to dinner at our Millsborough home. Samuel was pleased.

I'd met Nell at a public reading when I first came back to the area. Musical, broad, and deep, she and Jim reminded me of parents I never had. Charles and his partner, Nate, frequented a sandwich-and-pizza shop I'd enjoyed that featured local art and great brews. We'd wave at each other at the end of a hard workweek or as I confronted a momentous struggle of student papers. Later on we conversed and found we had a lot to say. And I'd respected and admired Old Sarah from the time I first saw her, a presence at lectures and forums and rallies (I only ever attended the one rally, my throat crushed around my heart) where the Iraq War was dissected and critiqued. Her arthritic hands wielded angry signs and importunate pens with youthful fervor. *I may be an old Sarah*, she'd say, *but I've got my voice and opinion same as the young ones.*

These friends came to eat at our table singly or together, and by the end of the meal and lingering visit, when we closed the door after our departing company, Samuel, though he didn't say much all night, would wear a softer face. The weight he carried in his limbs would have dissipated, and his voice roused with more ease. His steps were invigorated for several days afterwards.

We cleaned up the evening together and went to bed, a pleasurable undertaking.

I wanted to do more.

"Your friends," Samuel said, one night as we read together, without looking up from his book, "raise considered ideas. It's enlivening to hear."

I laid my own book face-down on my knees. "You know, we could raise our own little enclave of ideas. Right here, every week. Get everybody together for an evening of music and literature. Politics and history. Each of us could contribute something, and we could talk everything over, jam together, too, however we want." I was jarred by blurting this exciting notion. Curious if my excitement would transmit to the little growing being that now inhabited my body with me, I barreled on. "Lord, you know better than anyone, Samuel, there's a mighty land of philistines out there." In both our professions, my husband and I encountered the wearying effects of small-mindedness, of blight in its many forms. I turned toward him. "Why not do something more, even a small thing, together, to disrupt it?"

Samuel looked at me over the top of his book. He nodded and turned the page. "I'd certainly favor that."

He read on. I picked up my book again, cheered at my own cleverness.

Samuel was not an uncommonly happy man. Neither was he negative. He was shrewd, with an appraising eye, and here is how our relationship began to look to him: I had become a conduit of calm and intelligence, art and education, order and kindness into the house we shared. He appreciated the difference.

Naturally, this is my inference, based on careful study of what happened between us. It's how I understand his understanding of me, but it's also dangerous to assume that was ever the truth.

////// //// ////// // ////////

On an ordinary Tuesday night in March, our little community has gathered, and the evening is progressing with pleasantness and camaraderie.

Samuel sits in his recliner with a glass of wine and an expression that is focused and thoughtful. I've divorced my mind from the work waiting in my study upstairs. It's good to settle into a warm, laughing evening, with my little family, among friends.

Ian hums and mutters near the fireplace, with Giant the giraffe and an assortment of small plastic animals in his entourage. He's been asked already to divulge details of his day and to perform his garbled rendition of "Hickory Dickory Dock." When we clap, he beams and pulls his shirt tail up to his face. (His earlier shirt, soaked in apple juice and barbecue sauce from his pre-company supper, now lies on the washing machine. Likewise, his earlier splotchy, red, wet face—produced by copious weeping over homemade chicken nuggets, dumped into the floor—appears now only in the minds of Meredith and me.)

Meredith, who has been our faithful helper since our baby's birth, observes Ian and the rest of the room from the footstool where she always sits. She will not accept another seat.

Old Sarah has shaken her tambourine and recited the news from Iraq.

Charles has shared the first draft of a poem. Everyone's offered their thoughts, even Samuel, who usually declines to say much concerning poems. To me, the speaker in the poem seems off-kilter somehow. But I think that's Charles's intent.

Jim and Nell have played two rollicking new tunes and entertained us with the tales of how each piece was introduced to them.

The evening shines with a strong sheen.

Now Lorraine and I each will contribute our music for the evening, and afterward we will all jam together—Charles will extemporize along with us sometimes, too—until we grow tired enough to agree that the evening has ended.

Lorraine plucks a string, strums once, listens. "Here's something I worked with over the weekend." The smile that touches her face never fully forms. It suffuses her features.

She begins to play, and I am mesmerized.

Not only by the movement of her fingers. Nor by the sight of her surveying that agility with attentiveness, assurance. But the music holds me, and as I hear, I realize what she is playing. It is a story of water.

First the scattered, tentative drops. Then the rhythm of rain. Rush of rain. Bubble of wellspring, chuckle of creek, swell and torrent of river. I hear the river grow and spread and slow. A restful river. You could sit under a great tree on one of its banks and find calm. Healing.

It is like enchantment, really. How plain it is what she is playing.

Lorraine ends with a ripple eddying away.

We all applaud. Even Ian, who will soon be shuttled off to bed.

"Beautiful," says Charles.

"Well done," says Samuel.

"So you wrote that?" says Nell.

"I did."

"All those expressions of water," I say.

Lorraine smiles. "Yes, that's it, you could tell."

I am overjoyed. And now it is my turn.

I haven't had much time to practice this past week, so, on the dulcimer in my lap, I fingerpick a piece that's always moved me, a dipping, swaying waltz. I have no special musical ability, I know, but I am competent at this, moving my fingers across the strings, fretting the chords, causing Old Sarah to smile and nod with the tempo. It is gratifying to make my music.

Midway through, I hear a banjo burble up, and Lorraine is accompanying me.

I am perturbed.

This is not how we do things.

She's new and doesn't know.

She's been here enough to know.

I see my friends' faces brighten at the innovation. And all at once it feels like I am in a den of thieves.

It is a galvanizing, terrifying feeling.

I continue to play, and Lorraine does too. But I realize now the other faces in the room, including Samuel's, hold secrets from me.

And I'm certain that those secrets are about me.

My heart surges and overpowers all my thoughts.

I was right to doubt her. From the very first.

She's too familiar, cozying in my space, treating me like she knows me. Who does she think she is?

And emphatically I know that this insight, this power of discernment, is from God.

Of course it is.

Every nerve in my body is consumed in a great conflagration.

We finish the tune. Lorraine serves up her broad, wholesome, farm-girl smile, and the clapping for us is generous.

I speak before I can stop. "That banjo of yours sure has a lot to say, doesn't it?"

Somewhere, softly, I'm aware this is harsh of me.

"I'm afraid so." Lorraine turns to me, laughter in her voice. "I never know what to say, myself, but that lovely music of yours made me want to show how much I appreciated it. My banjo nearly jumped in all by itself."

My brain is burning, and the veins in my neck. *What's she really doing here?*

"That was a delightful choice," says Old Sarah.

"You both sounded great," says Jim.

I will choose to be mollified. I have a child to kiss good night, a husband who is looking at me with a touch of trouble in his eyes, and a roomful of guests counting on me to smooth the wrinkled surfaces of conversation so we can finish out the evening.

Who among them is not laughing at me in their minds?

"Thank you." I put something onto my face that I hope masquerades as grace. "Lorraine certainly brings a revelatory dimension to our tribal gatherings."

She's a new revelation to me, all right. All I can see is lit by her light.

She grins. "I'm glad you approve."

Her smile is open and free. I don't like it. It is a fearful thing to see.

///// //// ///// // ////////

The very first night Lorraine Davis had come to us, as she played her banjo, she had released every tone metallic and resonant to the air.

She rolled the notes one after another in smooth succession or bounced them high and low with drive and great energy.

She handled her instrument with deftness and certainty, and it repaid her with fire and liveliness.

Nell had lifted an eyebrow at me, spasmed her shoulders.

Lorraine appeared harmless. Competent.

Gifted, even.

Listening to her play, I'd felt taller. I'd felt lighter. As though it would be effortless to grade ten classes' worth of papers on two hours' sleep.

I could chase Ian, laughing, around the back yard, play hide and seek all over the house for a week of afternoons.

I had years of usefulness ahead of me, waiting like a container of eggs still unbroken, still holding the possibilities of quiche, egg salad, sunshine omelets.

Her music touched the weak and weary spots in me. Bloomed them into beauty.

Awash with wonderment, I'd reflected whether Lorraine's great wealth of heartfelt art might engender this effect only in me.

Or in everyone.

///// //// ///// // ///////

*B*efore God spoke to me in my study, this freshman who entered my office would have seemed a philistine to me. She hugged a textbook to her chest, a defensive move.

I was expecting her.

"Dr. Huffman? You said we could talk about my paper?"

Though I enjoyed my students, fraught consultations—such as this one would surely be—always challenged me. I put down my pen and moved my work to the side, clearing the space between us. "Absolutely. Come on in, Lindsey, have a seat."

"Thanks." She picked her way across the room and lowered herself onto the chair on the other side of the desk.

Whenever I encounter the philistines of the world, I've had trouble keeping my composure. The guy driving the pickup truck with the Confederate battle flag on the bumper sticker. The Rush Limbaugh devotee. Churchy women who are passionately against abortion but are also against food stamps and WIC, paid maternity leave, and a host of other initiatives meant to assist struggling mothers. When people like these do or say something to put East Tennessee or any part of Appalachia in the national spotlight—earning my homeland loud ridicule or condemnation or both—I grimace. I groan. I want to wear a paper bag over my head until the uproar subsides.

I want to holler so both coasts can hear me, "That's not the whole story around here!"

Lindsey settled her book in her lap. "Dr. Huffman, look, I just don't think my grade is very fair. I put a lot of work into that paper. I didn't put everything off until the last minute."

"I know. I could tell."

Her hand shoveled out, palm up. "So, what?—you mark me down because I put Bible verses in?"

From the instant I'd cringed at discovering what she'd done, I'd dreaded this conversation. "No, Lindsey, your grade was based on your lack of support for your paper's claim."

Her eyes and mouth both widened. Her hand dropped into her lap. "What're you talking about? I wrote about how horrible slavery was. I did the research. And I put in all those verses as evidence to show what God said he would do to people who were unjust and disobedient."

Hers had been the most original paper in my stack. But her critical mistake had left me with no choice but to give her a lower grade than I'm sure she wanted.

"Your *interpretation* of those verses is what's at issue," I said. "Because you state God's anger over the injustice of slavery is a root cause of the American Civil War, and then you quote the King James Bible as proof. Which is problematic for a number of reasons." I reminded myself to take a breath. "All of them having to do with the fact that your particular reading of those verses isn't supported by evidence in your paper. Frankly, I don't know if you *could* support such a reading."

She looked even more shocked, if that could be possible. "Why not?"

I rested my forearms on my desk, elbows out, to steady myself. I leaned toward her to indicate my interest and concern. "Well, to begin with, you'd have to show that the verses you quote—which were originally written in Hebrew—even refer to America, since their immediate context in their surrounding passages would suggest otherwise. And to prove that they do as you say, you'd have to work with the original Hebrew text—not a translation like the King James Bible—and also review existing scholarship about the interpretation of those verses. And in the end, even after you'd done all that—though I'm hardly a scholar of the Hebrew Bible—I still don't think you'll find that the writers you quote were writing about the situation in America."

She looked confused. "But the Bible is for everybody! Of course it's for America."

I had to pause before what I would say next. I'd wrestled mightily with Lindsey's paper because of the unscholarly assumption she'd made. Personally, I had trouble even seeing the Bible how she did—as universal, ahistorical truth—and I tended to mistrust and prejudge the people who did.

But now I was putting myself in the camp of faith. And the pastor of my new church talked about seeing others as if they were Jesus himself.

Nevertheless, my job was to teach this student about history scholarship.

"Lindsey, that's a faith claim. Not a thesis statement supported by research."

First she looked incredulous. Then she looked mean, her eyes constricted, her cheeks puffed like some bird's warning plumage. "So you did mark me down because I'm Christian."

It was impossible not to get angry. I did get angry.

"Lindsey, I did no such thing. I did not, and I would not." I fought to keep my voice even. "If you'd approached your subject from another angle—if, for instance, you had looked at what people at the time of the Civil War believed about God's involvement—then that would've made for a perfectly fine paper, because that's a subject that can be researched and your findings documented in your writing. You can show how research led you to your conclusion, whatever that might be." I sighed. "Your grade has nothing to do with the fact that you believe in God, or that you wanted to write about God in your paper. I thought you had an interesting argument, but unfortunately, it's extremely hard to support in a history assignment like that one."

"Wait—you thought my idea was interesting?"

She'd supplied what seemed an adjective I could own. "I did, yes."

Lindsey continued to blink at me. The sharpness faded from her eyes. "It's just—I'd heard it would be really tough coming to a non-Christian school. That some teachers want to scapegoat you if you're a person of faith. I'm sorry."

I nodded. "It can be challenging," I said, "coming into a new environment and not knowing what to expect."

I realized if I'd had this conversation even two months before, I would've disparaged this student in my head. Never out loud, never on paper, but—even though I'd always respected Mamaw and her faith experience—I would have maligned this young woman in my head for the rest of the term.

"Isn't there anything I can do about my grade?" she said. "Please, I really care about this class and my work."

I wondered if Lindsey might be the first in her family to attend college. I decided to extend a little mercy. "You can write something in your own words that explains back to me what I've just explained to you, what the error was you made in your paper. You'll need to convince me that you really understand, because the goal is that you learn about how historical research works. If you can turn that in to me in a week, giving a satisfactory explanation, then I'll raise your grade a letter on the assignment."

"Okay." She nodded. "I guess that's fair."

Lindsey was just as much a human being, I reminded myself, as the man whose tender ears I'd seen during that first church service. She was just as vulnerable, just as valuable. I did not see the world the way she did, but I was still enjoined to believe that she was loved.

"Thanks a lot, Dr. Huffman."

"Thanks, Lindsey, for coming by."

Immeasurably much.

///// //// ///// // //////

Already before Lorraine arrived that Tuesday in April, the evening felt heightened.

Everyone in the room, even Ian, seemed to crackle with the electricity of their thoughts. Everyone seemed to hold a mask of a face toward me.

I wondered if they were thinking about me and what they might be thinking.

I'd rummaged up an afghan for Old Sarah and was just settling her in her seat with it when Lorraine knocked. So Nell went to get the door.

Lorraine entered the room and headed straight for Ian. She carried a box covered in balloon-print paper and was bent forward a little, so her eyes were nearer to his.

Ian squealed. "Me, Lorraine?" Her name sounded like *Wayne* in his mouth.

"Yes, it *is* for you!" Lorraine offered the box into his hands.

Ian's birthday didn't happen until October.

We'd never once hinted to anyone in our circle they should bring gifts to our child.

"Goodness, Lorraine," said Charles, "you're showing us up."

I was shocked. Angered by Lorraine's impudence. Suspicious.

In the most rapid succession.

"Mommy!" Ian lifted the box between us. "Looky!"

I couldn't help but see.

"You didn't have to do that." I moved closer to Lorraine. All my mind could contain was a screeching whirl.

She was way, way too much.

Lorraine shrugged and produced one of her winning smiles. "It was no trouble. Just a little thing."

My son had plopped the box onto his lap. He dug at the bright, balloon-covered paper. Jagged strips ripped away.

"Mrs. Davis," said Samuel, "I'm sure that's very thoughtful of you."

Lorraine sort of ducked her head. "I saw it at checkout the other day, and I couldn't resist." She watched the box emerging amid the shreds of paper.

I was watching, too.

In a voice meant for Ian, Jim said, "So, what you got there?"

Ian grunted. "Not get." He pried at the stubborn lid.

"You need help, son?" said Samuel.

Only then I realized I was standing close by while Ian struggled. "Here, baby." I knelt and ran my finger through the gap between box and lid, popping the small strip of tape. It discouraged me to do that. "Try it now."

He plunged his hands into waves of tissue paper and pulled out a woolly, floppy, stuffed creature, a lamb. His face opened like the gift.

I heard the appreciative sounds from our friends.

"Oh!" Ian turned his toy this way and that. In a blur, he hugged the lamb hard against him.

Ian had always loved animals, pretend and real. Her present was perfection.

"Can you say thank you?" I said. As far as I was concerned, there was no other means by which thanks would be given. It would not come out of my mouth.

Ian's eyes were shut, his body curved down over the lamb. "Thank you, Lorraine."

"You're welcome, little buddy." Almost in a tone of apology, she said, "It made me think of him."

In that minute I understood I would have to throw a fence up all around my house, forever keep the curtains closed. Since when did this woman know what my son loved? When had she discovered his favorite sandwich, the plastic tugboat and family of ducks that shared his bath time, his happy sigh when I turned out the light and galaxies of glowing stars flashed on to cover his bedroom ceiling?

No one else in the room seemed to notice what she was doing—though their thoughts seemed bent my way again tonight—but her intention came to my mind in towering, incinerating letters—*she had come to usurp me.*

///// //// ///// // ///////

*S*amuel was asleep, but I was not. He breathed contentedly. I was seething in the dark.

I could not see how Lorraine could get away with her antics, her conniving against me, in a room full of people who were supposed to be my friends. My family, for Christ's sake. How nobody could notice what she was doing.

Where was the love that had filled my heart, suffused my body? I was supposed to forgive her. Was I a monster?

I stared at the clock. 1:38. I stared at the bedroom door.

Then I slipped from under the covers. Samuel stirred, then stilled.

I left the room and padded down the hall to my study. My heart thudded the tempo of my thinking.

What Lorraine intended was palpable. It was as clear as a Windexed window.

She contrived to crowd me out of my circle.

I closed the door and switched on the desk lamp. I sank onto the loveseat. I huddled forward with lowered head and tried to pray.

I was a wretched person. Lorraine was a guest each week in my home. Our heavenly banjo player. Her husband worked at the courthouse with Samuel.

Her machinations against my little son were blatant.

I needed God to show me what to do. "Please," I whispered. The house was so very silent. "Please. I need answers."

I waited. Nothing.

I lifted my head. Searched the spines of my books on the bookcases.

I was supposed to write a book.

That was it.

I had been flooded with light, soaked in awareness and insight.

God would reveal through the writing of the book what I was meant to learn. There was nothing Lorraine did that did not have significance. As I documented each detail, this book would prove instructional to me. And to others later, perhaps.

I could feel the anxiety dropping away from me like heavy fabric. I did not know what *new ways* I would discover, but I could surely *declare* what I was given.

I rummaged through a desk drawer for notebook and pen. Barefoot, I curled on the loveseat and began to write.

I, Susan Huffman, have been given a word from God. A word and a warning.

It was good to set this down. I was pleased and relieved.

I write so the acts of Lorraine may be remembered and the truth made evident.

I plunged on. I wrote for fifteen minutes, twenty minutes, more.

The study door clicked. Creaked. I shut the book. I thought I had woken Ian somehow.

But it was Samuel. "Is everything all right?"

I'd been so engrossed in writing, I hadn't heard the squeak of the floor in the hall. "Oh, yes," I said. I didn't want to worry him with my problem. When I finished the book, that would be the time for revelation.

He hesitated, then edged on into the room through a widening door, which he shut very carefully behind him.

I felt protective. I felt annoyed. There was so much to write. I wanted to write.

Samuel shuffled in his blue and white striped pajamas toward the desk like a bear waking from winter sleep. He turned the chair to face me and occupied it. His big hands curved down the armrests.

This man filled my life with good things. I loved making love to this man. I didn't understand why God wanted me not to confide in him.

"You've seemed troubled lately," Samuel said. "What is it? Your tenure review?"

Tenure review was a mirage in a dream. "Could be. That could be it."

I had to trust that God knew my situation better than I did. The writing of my book would be an exercise in faith.

Samuel appraised me with his incisive eyes. "If you need Meredith to come and help more, we can do that. And I'll certainly do what is in my power to do, to arrange things around here to make them as easy for you as I can. Ian's bedtimes and outings, too, if that will help."

I nodded. I felt woeful to lose out on any more of Ian's bedtimes and outings than I already did. But I supposed it was not realistic to expect otherwise. "Thank you, Samuel."

He leaned toward me and rested his hand on my knee. His eyes stayed steady on my face. "You're a strong woman, Susan. Intelligent. Thorough. There's no reason on earth why you shouldn't come through all right."

I had to respond some way. I pressed my hand on top of his. "Thank you. Your confidence means a lot." With Lorraine's scheming infiltrating every part of my life, I would have to take special care with my husband. I kissed the place where his jawline met with his neck and his ear. "Let's go back to bed."

////// //// ////// // ////////

Oh what a beautiful world it was that day.

My baby and I heading home with a car full of groceries.

A car full of spring. A car full of blessings.

Praise music soared around me from the stereo speakers. My heart was bigger than the sky.

On that bright blue day, ablaze with sun, as we approached the man with the sign that read, "No car – No work – God bless," I knew what God wanted from me. The certainty bubbled up behind my ribs.

The unkempt stranger could be Jesus. The Bible taught me this.

I stopped the car.

The man was watching me now.

I would do what God asked. I would not be deterred by what others might think or say. I turned down the volume and lowered the passenger side window. "Sir, do you need a ride somewhere?"

"Hey, don't everybody?"

"Mommy?" said Ian. "Song on."

"There's a resource center downtown," I said, "that can help out with jobs. Other things, too. I can drop you down there, if you want." It was not so late in the afternoon. They'd have to be open until five.

The man shrugged. "Not like there's some other place wanting me."

"Okay." I unlocked the doors. "Climb in."

The man hesitated. Coming closer, he pulled the door open and sat in the front seat. He brought his sign with him and an overwhelming stench. The door was shut, and I pulled away from the curb.

"Me song, Mommy," said Ian. "Song on."

The man glanced at me out of eyes tight and hard.

"In a minute, baby," I said. "We're taking this nice man downtown, okay?"

The man made a scoffing noise. "Lady, you ain't got no idea about me at all."

"You're right. I don't." The unfamiliar presence in the car jostled the bright expanse I'd felt inside me. I tried to recover. "Are you from Millsborough?"

"I'm from everywhere. Seems like. But, yeah, that, too."

I kept steadying the wheel, turning the wheel, taking us through traffic. "I was born in Millsborough myself, but did most of my growing up in Clemtown."

"Lord, hell, you sure don't sound like no Clemtown. Sound like some rich Yankee to me."

"Well. I'm not."

"No fight," said Ian.

My son's comment flummoxed me. I'd thought there existed only a cool sort of cheerfulness in my voice.

The man pivoted then to look at Ian, and my heart kicked very high.

"Hey, no fighting here, little man. Everybody's just talking."

I realized I was shaking. For the first time, I wondered if the man might have a knife, a gun.

For the first time, I wondered if God might be asking us to die.

"This? Who this?" Ian asked, sounding confused.

The man said, "I am Dirty Harry, sonny boy. Y'all can go ahead and make my day." He gave me a grim smile of bad teeth. "Bet you didn't know that, huh, lady? You didn't know I'm a big-shot movie star right here in Millsborough." He winked at me, slow and sly, before turning toward the windshield again.

"No, I sure didn't." It was now hard to think of anything coherent to say.

"Yeah, boy." The man chuckled. "World famous, that's me. Right here."

Two more lights, and we would be at the resource center. "Well, for right now, maybe the folks at the center can help you out with some job prospects." I was now praying in my head. I sounded like an idiot. All I'd wanted was to treat this pitiful, scary-crazy man like Jesus, to do what God had asked me to do.

"Never knew I had me any *pros-pects*." The man ground down on the word. "Wow. Reckon I need me a whole lot more of them."

I put on the turn signal. "I hope you can find whatever you need." Here was the place. There were cars in the parking lot.

"You know what, lady? Same to you."

I let him out at the entrance. He started to shut the car door, but leaned inside a moment more.

"Little man, back there, you listen up. Your mama here, she don't know shit about nothing. But she's trying to do right. Don't you forget that."

I couldn't say what I felt in that mixed-up moment.

"Okay, bye," said Ian.

"Good luck," I said.

I didn't wait to see if the man actually went in the building or not. When he began walking away, I drove on, in a car full of groceries, back to my house with my little boy.

We didn't turn the music back up for a block or two.

"Dirty Harry all gone," said Ian.

Later that evening, at supper, Ian would inform Samuel I had fought with Dirty Harry earlier in the day. "This, this nice man. Stinky."

After my further explanation, Samuel would raise an eyebrow. "Are you sure that's such a good idea? With Ian in the car?"

I still would not have satisfactorily resolved for myself how great the danger had been. "It seemed right at the time." Still using my fork, I would open my other hand, releasing the finished event to the sky.

But I would know what I had believed, that God had asked me to give that man a ride. It had felt good to acquiesce, and it had been terrifying, too. And I would know that I would pray that God would never, ever, ask me to do such a crazy thing in my life ever again.

////// //// ////// // ///////

I am mystified why so many of my friends cannot see that you, God, are the one working in my life to transform me. They are suspicious. Shake their heads and tell me how mistaken I am. They prefer the old Susan to the one that is now being molded by you. But the Bible says this is not an uncommon reaction. In fact, it says that your followers can expect to be persecuted. So I won't let myself become discouraged. Instead I will strive to look to you for comfort and peace.

When I share this book with the world, I pray that people will be transformed by it just as I have been—and am being— transformed by you. That they will see how much they are loved. That there is a power that cares deeply about what happens to them. That the universe is working toward an ending of triumph and glory. That the greatest crisis, the greatest failure, is no match for the might of your love and your life and your healing.

Yet every time Lorraine comes to our house, I have trouble believing in goodness. In your ability to love everyone the same. Every time she enters, our house becomes a place of shadows and whispers. I want to hate her because of this, but you command me otherwise.

And still I hate her. I can't get rid of the fear and the hate.

Not even Samuel can understand what I am about. Is this because of the man that he is? How he is made? Or is his doubt in me thanks to Lorraine and her banjo?

And yet—you are the one who shows me all that she does. It has to come from you. So how am I supposed to respond? I don't know how you want me to make use of that knowledge.

Unless you mean for the knowledge to make use of me.

////// //// ////// // ////////

One morning I opened my eyes and discovered that the distance from the bed to the shower was greater now than the distance from Millsborough to Alpha Centauri.

A dark ache dripped through my blood and bathed my bones.

I believed my bed would swallow me, and no one would ever think to search for me there, not even Samuel, and I would never be found.

I was immobile. I wanted to be nowhere.

I had been blue on a rainy day. I had been a weeping mess of hormones in the weeks after Ian's birth. But I had never, never found myself in a place like this. I had never thought it was possible for me.

I dragged myself to my feet with all the willpower I possessed.

Samuel just tied his tie and did not seem to notice my trouble. I was grateful.

I was ten thousand miles from the nearest soul.

I forced myself under the shower head and the hard fall of hot water.

I had easily, effortlessly gotten out of bed and taken a shower every day of my life, unless I'd been stricken by some dire sickness.

I went through that whole day feeling each step I took could be my last, and I would just stop, wherever I was, forever.

In that gray endlessness.

////// //// ////// // ////////

After a sunny, sweaty day at the park—which I have welcomed, a vibrant day—Ian is snuggling his Lorraine-gifted lamb, tucked next to him in the crib. He looks up at me and smiles.

I've pushed my son on the swings. I've fed him his cheese sandwich and Goldfish. I've taken him for ice cream afterward.

I'm sharing this moment with him.

From my son, out of nowhere, comes the satisfied and glowing declaration, "Lorraine smiles me, Mommy."

And there is the final word on this day.

In reply, my hand touches the top of his head. I stroke-smooth his hair.

I've wanted all my life to have anyone say such kind, loving things about me. But I have turned out neither kind nor loving.

///// //// ////// // ////////

On a regular day, Ian and I are like this:

His bag is already filled with Kleenex, napkins, hand sanitizer, and, just in case, an extra change of underwear and clothes. He's allowed to take a toy with him that he likes, but I never let him take one that is particularly prized, like Giant. I'm concerned about it being maimed or lost. I will make him a cheese and mayonnaise sandwich, most likely, and also pack milk, Goldfish, and some fruit cocktail, in one hundred percent juice, along with a plastic spoon. Sometimes as a treat, I put in some hamburger dill pickle chips.

(I am not enthusiastic about Ian's insistence on mayonnaise, but have learned to relent. It's what he loves on his sandwich. I can give him a little.)

Ian's daycare is on the road that leads out of town and to Edenton and the college. Samuel takes Ian on those rare mornings when I arrive on campus late. Otherwise I drive my little son. I hoist Ian into and out of the car. I strap him snugly in his car seat, unfasten the straps to set him free. He watches my hands as I move them. Sometimes he looks in my face. This devastates me. I can hardly bear to see him then, trusting me because he knows no other possibility. He knows no better.

Leaving him there, in that building with the colorful walls and the cheery ladies and the noisy children, is the hardest thing I will do all day.

In the afternoons, I usually am the one who collects Ian and his inscrutable fingerpaintings of fish and birds, hears his enthusiastic and disjointed recountings of his day as we travel the road home. Meredith will meet us there, where the supper chores will begin. But when I have a late meeting, Meredith drives my child back to the house. The first time this happened, when Ian was four months old, I thought I would hyperventilate all through my discussion with Dr. Rickwell. Now I simply don't think about it. That's what's best, because I can't.

At home, Meredith and I take turns cooking and playing. Ian laughs, his face breathtakingly beautiful, or becomes cranky and hungry and weepy. Now is not the time for me to remember the plentitude of exams or research papers in the bag in my study upstairs. Ian builds tall, spindly towers of alphabet blocks, makes toy cats and dogs and elephants parade through the living room, listens to a CD of children's songs and sings along, messing up the words. Or Ian wails and clings to my legs.

Except on Tuesdays, Meredith leaves once Samuel arrives. No matter how wearied and exasperated the day has rendered my husband, Samuel and Ian are glad to be reunited, at this moment—for five minutes, ten—this sacred spot of time that is never as long as they wish.

Ian and I have our own moments like this, and so I know.

Samuel listens to Ian tell about his day, asks me how my own day went. He never says much about the hours he spends in the courtroom, the issues brought to him in chambers. He, too, has a sheaf of papers, stashed somewhere, that he will get to work through later.

Ian generally eats without fussiness. After supper, I fix him a slice of buttered toast and honey. Ian is wild for honey. It is worth the sticky shirts and fingers to hear him smack his lips as he eats, to observe the shining approval in his eyes.

Samuel and I take turns—nightly most often, but week-about sometimes—putting supper away. The one who restores order to our kitchen and family dining space will disappear into his or her study shortly following, and that one will also stand the best chance of getting to bed at a sensible hour. The other of us shepherds Ian through what remains of the evening and accepts the late-night shift.

When it's my turn to supervise Ian's bath time and bedtime, he is giggly and giddy. Or he's sullen and falling asleep on his feet. He likes nursery rhymes and books with droning rhythms for bedtime reading. He snuggles in my lap as we contour ourselves into the rocking chair in his room. Sometimes he helps to chant the books along with me. I smell the mild, sweet smell of his hair. His body gets heavy with sleep. I want to hold him there the rest of the night. For many years together.

I want my son to know a childhood with no resemblance to mine.

Too soon, I tuck him beneath the covers, behind the safety of the rail. I extinguish the light on this day.

///// //// ///// // ///////

The stuffed lamb from Lorraine, which I'd called Lammykin right from the start, had gone nearly gray after being hauled wherever Ian went. The lamb came to all meals, romped with my son in the yard. Ian even defied—with Samuel's support, no less—my prohibition against taking beloved toys to daycare.

Though in this case, I wouldn't have minded if the lamb had been lost.

"Lammykin," I said to Ian, "needs a bath."

That curly-haired, blue-eyed, mouthless creature would not leave my head. It was lying in wait for me, always, churning my thoughts. Between classes. During office hours. As I drove about Millsborough. Whether I tried to sleep or awoke in the night.

And of course, whenever I saw my son, because the lamb was always there, throttled in the crook of his arm.

The toy gaped at me with enormous eyes. It only seemed innocent. Because whenever that lamb entered my mind, it dragged Lorraine along with it.

Ian's forehead furrowed. "No. He clean. Me, too."

"Uh-huh," I said. "We'll see about that."

Ian clutched the floppy animal tighter. "Lammykin no want to."

"Lamkin" was a poem from an undergraduate English class that I sort of remembered, one of those medieval ballads we studied. The ghastly rhyming story of a home intruder who murdered a wife and baby, all because of some wrong done him by the husband. To me, the title made a fitting name for my son's pet "lamby."

I held out my hand. "Ian," I said. "He'll have a chance to dry, and you can have him back in time for bed. Come on. Give him to me."

Ian stomped and whimpered. I had not thought this through. I should have sneaked Lammykin out of Ian's room in the middle of the night. I reached to pry the toy away. My son slung it at me and cried harder.

"It's okay. Here's Giant," I said, quickly. "It won't be long."

So Lammykin and I headed for the laundry. Samuel was outside mowing the yard. With the windows open, the house was fragrant and mellow with the scent of fresh-cut grass. I took down a small plastic tub and pulled out a bottle of Woolite, which had its own fresh and bubbly smell. I poured soap and water into the plastic tub and dunked the detested toy into it. I began scrubbing suds against the cloth of the body.

But my thoughts would not stay on the washing.

How could Lorraine be so very earnest and open, and at the same time carry with her a secret as big as anything? I could see her face right then. She would make a merry twitch with her eyebrow, and that sweep of smile followed. You could not help but love her. The reach of her eyes was as inclusive as anyone could wish.

My breathing came harder. I bore down on the lamb. The grime released into the water.

I could see all the evenings with Lorraine. Each turn of her head, every arched brow. Every bubble of laughter escaping her lips. The dazzle of music she made.

Moments exchanged between Lorraine and Ian, between Lorraine and Samuel.

Between Lorraine and me.

My mind was careening. I held onto the lamb and dumped out the tub of sudsy water.

I could see the secret. I could tell what lurked behind Lorraine's face.

I was not going to be loved.

It hurt my heart to think of what I would lose.

The sodden, white face regarded me as I returned the lamb to the tub and ran fresh water in. The blue plastic eyes glinted.

It was laughter in her eyes. Was it laughter in her eyes?

I stopped the water. Every nerve in me was stripped of its sheath. Every nerve was on fire. I yanked the dripping animal from the tub. Heat exploded behind my eyes. I could not tolerate this goddamned smirking lamb one minute more. I twisted the creature's head to try and pull it off. When the head stayed stuck, I began slamming the stupid thing against the wall. Hoping to bash in its face. The lamb sprayed water all over me.

That woman wanted my son. She wanted the entirety of my life. I was covered in rage.

The lamb's eyes knocked loose and struck against the floor, plastic clicks scattering. The toy was blind now. I flung it down in a soggy heap. Heaving with breathing, I looked where it lay.

It was dead. My gloating turned to horror.

What I'd done would become known. And right then. Scuffling little feet were coming through the kitchen. There was no time to go for the glue.

"Mommy?" Ian bounded in, hopeful. "He dry?"

There was no time, nothing to say to interpret for Ian what he was going to see. Was in fact seeing there at my feet.

"My Lammykin!" My child collapsed on the ground. Scooped the wet bundle of synthetics and cotton against his chest and cried. Howled the name he called me. I have no word for the hideous, piteous bellowing he made.

I was crying, too, now. Terrified, I dropped to the floor on my knees and reached for my son. His body resisted, an awful instant, but he crumpled into me. His face burned against my shoulder. It would not stop scalding me.

"Shhh." I rocked and patted him. "We'll glue his eyes back, and he'll be better soon." Somehow I had to explain what I could not. "Poor Lammykin had a bad accident."

"You letted!" Ian jerked with his words to emphasize his vehemence. "Mommy see Lammykin fall."

"I know you love him, and Mommy will fix him. Mommy's so sorry. So sorry."

We huddled together there and wept. Ian was a child of warmth and salt water in my arms. I was made of mud, thick and noxious. I was built of air, so insubstantial I could barely find myself.

A little voice tucked into a quiet corner made an astute observation—*something was very wrong with me.*

////// //// ////// // ////////

My mind had revolved through the laundry room a thousand times. I'd taught, held office hours, spoken with colleagues, while destroying Ian's lamb during every bit of it.

I'd driven to lunch and not once had I turned my son loose.

"Do you mind if I pray before we eat?" I said to Nell. I craved all the help I could get.

"Not at all." Nell set her fork down in a gesture like an afterthought, as if the utensil had needed some artful rearranging. "Go right ahead."

I closed my eyes and asked God to bless our food and our conversation. I asked God for good counsel. "Amen," I said.

Nell said, "Yes."

We started eating our salads. Nell had arrived at the restaurant late. She always did. I had a class at two.

"I've been terribly short with Ian." It wasn't exactly what I'd done but was near enough. To put into words what was in my head I thought would destroy me. The tines of my fork clicked against my plate. "I can't condone it, I don't believe in acting that way." Lorraine was taking over my mind.

"Well, if you don't believe in it, don't do it. That's not good for you. Or for anyone." Nell chewed a moment. "Are there changes you can make, more sleep or something?"

"Not much, not really. Not now." I could not find the least love in my heart for the fall symposium. That project buried itself beneath the divine book I wrote. My tenure review was tearing toward me. I sawed a piece of chicken. "I need to work on my anger, I guess."

"Will you tell me something if I ask you?" Nell's wood bangles clanked together.

I rested my knife on the edge of the plate. I nodded.

"Are you feeling all right these days?"

"Today?" The idea of answering her exhausted me. Mamaw would have said *it wore me slap out.* "No, I feel pretty wretched. Frantic, anxious. But most days, sure, I feel fantastic. Like I'm right where God wants me to be."

I didn't mention those days when I couldn't take showers.

Nell drank sweet tea, returned her glass to the table. "Anyone would want to be in such a spot, the place we're meant to be. Sometimes I think I'm there, waking up in sunshine, drinking my slow cup of coffee. You know me."

Nell was the consummate late-riser. If I stayed in bed past nine, I would feel I had slept the day away. I put my hands in my lap. "I absolutely do. And I know you didn't ask me this for no reason."

In truth, I was having trouble making it all add up myself.

"Susan," she said, so gently I was even more suspicious, "if you're worried, afraid, wrestling with stress or maybe anger, then maybe you should get that checked out, don't you think?"

My throat turned very cold. "What, you're telling me I'm some kind of mental case now?" I couldn't believe her insinuation. I could not be having a breakdown. My life made too much sense.

Nell looked hurt. "I'm telling you no such thing. That's a hideous term, and I repudiate it. There's no harm in the world in seeking some life help if you're having a hard time navigating on your own. I'm sure there are some fine Christian counselors out there, or I have a friend I could refer you to."

This friend, I realized, could be Nell's own therapist. My response should be sensitive to the possibility. And Nell was my friend, a brilliant fiddler and a deeply authentic woman, whom I admired for her life lived centered in her convictions. To her, life was an exercise in trust, and she believed the universe answered faithfully. Instead I had always trusted in the power of my own mind.

Until God showed up.

"Thank you," I said. "That's good of you, Nell, it really is."

I saw a wavering like disappointment, like an image on water, in her eyes. "Naturally. I want you to be all right," she said.

I picked up my glass. I wasn't all right, but her proposal seemed extreme to me. I still had a grip on my mind. "I just don't think I'm quite to that point yet," I explained.

But I wondered how I would know when I had gotten there.

///// //// ///// // ///////

If, in February of 2002, two months after our marriage, I'd gone to Samuel and told him I couldn't have a child, not then, we would've terminated the pregnancy. I know we would. But when I told my husband I was pregnant, I had already made my choice.

The day I confirmed the reason for my missing periods, I left the doctor's office and drove down to the river on an exquisite afternoon, more perfect than could ever be expected for a winter's day. I walked in the park there along the riverbank, a dark heaviness in my chest, and the mountains seemed very near. They were gray and bared and looked like eternity on earth more than anything I have ever witnessed. My mind was everywhere, which made it hard to see. I traveled one end of the path to the other, and then I began again. The wind was brisk. The sun was warm. I walked by the river until I could find my body once more, my arms and legs, my head. I walked until my mind was still.

I lived by my mind. I could weigh options, analyze, synthesize, bring my mind to bear, make it up in a trice. People are always pontificating about listening to your heart, and maybe that is wisdom of a sort, but I was not going to choose without my mind.

I sat on a park bench and watched the few people wander past me who were out on a weekday afternoon. The shadows lengthened, and sunlight burnished the earth. My mind stayed quiet. An elderly couple walked by, arms linked, the woman fidgeting with the man's shirt collar. I had a sense of the slow earth's turn, the unyielding years. My mind fixed on the notion that my life was unfolding, and the years of it turned in one direction only. My work was extremely important to me. I felt a purpose in my research, a purpose in instilling knowledge in the young people in this part of the world.

The world was a much bigger thing than I was, though. There was so much to experience. I did not know if I was cut out to be anyone's mother. Most of what I'd learned from my own mother, who rarely occupied the same waking room with me, was how to work hard. I did not know if I was strong and brave and resourceful enough to further my career while rearing a child.

Marrying Samuel hadn't been part of my life plan once, either.

I sat until the land began to darken. The river flashed as it swirled and pushed along. The mountains remained where they were.

I got up from the bench. I walked back to the car. I drove home to my husband.

By the time I entered the house, I thought I was being open. Willing to admit that my life could go a different way. It was hard, otherwise, to explain the decision I reached.

Samuel was gratified by the news. Dr. Rickwell said she supported me.

In the end, I wanted to try. I wanted the chance to try.

I still struggle daily with the consequences of my choice.

////// //// ////// // ////////

On an evening in early May, I was in pajamas, barefoot, curled on the loveseat in my study, reading my Bible, with my notebook of writings beside me. It'd been a difficult day, one of those when I could barely move. Meredith had stayed long enough to put Ian to bed and gone home.

Out of the quiet, the stairs mumbled beneath my husband's feet. The hallway creaked once, twice, and that was when I understood he was coming here.

I didn't know what I could even say. I was unsure if my mouth would make the words.

Samuel tapped the door once, then opened it before I could invite him in. "Susan, I'd like a word with you, please." His tone was neutral enough. Carefully so.

I set the Bible on the notebook. "Of course." I shifted, moved my legs to put my feet on the floor and offer the loveseat to him. It was an effort to do this.

He came and stood over me, his back to the desk. "Could you kindly explain what is going on with you these days?"

I lowered my head. "I wish I could, Samuel." I didn't know why I couldn't try harder at work, why I was so drained when I should be joyful, angry when I should be at peace. I had to be the worst and most slacking of all God's followers.

"Could you elaborate for me?"

I closed my eyes. "Everything hurts. I don't know why."

"What do you mean everything hurts?" There was an edge, a rush to his voice, "You should see a doctor if that's the case."

"I don't know what to tell the doctor. It's like I ache with the flu. It comes and goes. I take my temperature, and there's no fever."

Samuel didn't speak right away. "I think those would be reasonable grounds for a medical exam."

I nodded, my lids over my eyes still, so that I looked into darkness. "Probably. Yes."

"You can relay your symptoms to him as competently as you have to me."

"Maybe so."

"I have no doubt." There was another pause, and then his voice came much closer to me. "Let's get to the bottom of this. I think it would be in everyone's interest here."

My eyes opened, and I saw Samuel bending down with the same face he'd always had.

Which bewildered me far more.

"Yes," I said. "You're right."

"Ian wants you better," he said. "And so do I."

My head was stuffed full of soggy socks. "I'll make an appointment in the morning." I could not reconcile all of Samuel's sentences as coming from the same man.

///// //// ///// // //////

I saw the doctor. The doctor saw me and prescribed an antidepressant.

I was not used to the idea of medicine every day as an ongoing treatment for an underlying condition. But I did understand the need for homework, assignments to be completed for the student's own good. I recognized the analogy. So I took my medicine religiously as prescribed. The world became a shiny, aluminum-foil-glazed landscape beneath skies of July. In May.

Except when it wasn't.

Except on those days when the danger and rage and sadness hunted me, and I could not be still, and I wished to claw out the eyes of everyone I met, and I drove like the devil.

Those days shocked me with their many moments of terror.
God fled me on those days.
And I believed I was to blame.

I was walking across campus toward the end of exam week,
after lunch, headed to my office. The weather was radiant.
Glorious. The songs of birds like the sweetest of liquids, like
a fine rain of iced tea. But I was parched. The ordinary noise
of traffic, the relentless chatter of students vaulted at me from
every side. Reached me from the vast distance.

I had to pull away. The noise would obliterate me otherwise.
Flay every scrap of flesh from my skeleton. My insides were
shrieking.

I saw the fire escape on the outside of the science building. I
had passed it a thousand times before.

I started up it.

I climbed to the top, to the landing beneath the upper windows.
Up there was a metal railing I held to. Up there I perused the
high branches of trees and the topmost parts of buildings. Up
there the life of campus knotted and swayed below me.

As I looked down, I saw one possibility I'd never considered.

It was heart-poundingly simple to imagine myself sprawled
on the ground below. My stomach crushed as I pictured the fall.
The horrifying ease of it.

I tried to absorb this idea, as two students were walking the
path by the building.

One glanced up.

Lindsey.

Our eyes met. She halted.

I didn't move or think anything.

"Dr. Huffman?" I heard the astonishment in her voice. The other student stopped, too.

I remembered my husband. I remembered my son. "Hello, Lindsey." I tried to make the situation seem the most natural of moments.

"What're you doing?"

"Taking a long look around. Good to do sometimes."

"Sure." She sounded doubtful. "You do that a lot up there?"

"No," I had to admit. "There's a first time for everything, though."

Both students stayed looking up at me.

This was an embarrassment and a relief together. I couldn't evade their response.

There was nothing for me to do but return to the ladders and come down.

///// ////   ///// // ///////

When the church I attended took up offerings on Sundays, I'd begun by putting nothing into the baskets. I didn't owe anything, it seemed to me.

After I'd been a few times, I put a dollar in. A couple of dollars. Later I wanted to do more. I gave five dollars, ten.

One week, after exams and my excursion up the fire escape, just before the band began to play during the offering, the preacher told the rapt congregation that a special collection was being taken to buy supplies for a safe house for battered women and their children.

Where I sat in the dark, surrounded by so many sympathetic strangers, the plea unlatched the top of my head like a window. Sunlight and fragrant air gushed into me, firing up my brain and bursting into my eyes.

Some of the money, the preacher said, would go for necessaries, but some would be used for books, toys, wall art, and other items to make the place more inviting.

God had told me I could declare new ways. Why not new ways for desperate women? This chance was meant for me.

It felt like my chest had cracked open, because I could not contain the power and purity of the feeling that rose up and poured out of me.

I stood up. I pierced the clouds. "Yes, praise God! Let's help as hard as we can!"

Shouts and murmurings from elsewhere echoed what I'd said. People were looking at me. Were people looking? I had skin lacquered over in boldness. Maybe this was the kind of transformation that took place in God's followers that the Bible talked about.

I sat down again. I floated down. I was electric with the shock and tremble of my outburst. It felt absolutely right.

This time, before I passed the basket on, I dropped in a check for five hundred dollars.

God was on my side, and I was on God's. I had nothing to fear.

///// ////   ///// // ////////

"Susan, hey, I want to talk with you."

I put my pen down and closed the notebook. I should not have come to campus. But Ian was at a day out program—his daycare was closed for the summer—and I had the day to myself, so I'd brought a sandwich and my book to listen to God and write outdoors in the deserted place. Now I had to be patient and listen to Hugh—why was he here?—because that was the right thing to do.

"Is something going on?" he said. "You haven't been answering my e-mails. We need to firm up the schedule. Like, weeks ago. Get it out there and on the website, with the abstracts."

"I'm sorry, Hugh, I've had a lot to sort through lately."

A sharp look crossed his face. "What do you mean? What's the matter?"

He seemed like a man I'd been introduced to long ago, one I had a hard time recalling how I knew. I tried to smile. "Nothing to bother you with." It wasn't time to reveal Lorraine's deceit yet. I still was listening for when that would be.

"Because I have to tell you, Susan, you don't sound like yourself."

I was being made new by God. I was going to be who I was meant to be. "Well, I think it's important to try to work on myself now."

He folded his arms. "So is there a time we can meet up? Maybe tomorrow?"

"Hugh, I'm sorry, I just don't think that's how I'm supposed to spend my time tomorrow. We'll meet up soon and work all the details out."

I could not get excited about abstracts or websites. It was strange to think there was once a life in which I cared about those things.

Hugh made an exasperated sound, waved his hands in the air. "You need serious help, you know that? You are definitely not *being* one."

And off he charged.

I tried to locate the regret I ought to feel.

///// //// ////// // ////////

*T*uesday night, I was more brilliant and beautiful than I'd been since I could remember. Meredith and I made smoked salmon and cream cheese on rye toasts and brie in puff pastry. There was sliced fruit, and marinated cucumbers, and everything came out impossibly perfect, and I changed into a new green dress, which had cost a lot of money.

Ian ate his plate without too much fuss. Samuel came home and let me know right away how good I looked.

As our guests began to arrive, the grin inside of me was too large to fit on my face. So I kept it in, stretched wide, and nudged it from time to time.

Lorraine was going to know her place. Lorraine was going to know what it was to take me on.

My head, my whole body brimmed with the singing warmth of blood.

I covered the earth, and the smile inside of me did, too.

Tuesday night, I was more myself than even I was.

Everyone had played or performed. Everyone had opined and bantered, and Ian had gone to bed.

I was mostly satisfied.

Though everyone had remarked on my dress, Lorraine had gushed more.

I'd said I found it on the sale rack, which was true.

Though everyone raved about the food, Lorraine praised it more.

I said Meredith was the fabulous cook. True as well.

Though I'd answered in ways that the East Tennessee code of politeness required, I enjoyed the compliments all the same, knowing I would receive credit for making good choices.

But the evening carried an aftertaste, a lingering sense that my triumph was not certain. The grin inside me faltered and began to fade.

"Well, now, isn't it high time we had one of our parties?" said Old Sarah.

And just like that, I was intrigued by possibilities she'd laid out before me. My interior smile waited.

Charles' face brightened. "That would be marvelous."

"Do you and Samuel need help getting that together?" said Nell. "Because I can."

"Or we could do potluck," said Jim.

"Ooh, that would be different," Charles said.

I looked to catch Samuel's eye, but Samuel was already looking at me. "I think we can manage," I said to Nell and the others. "What do everyone's calendars look like?"

Nell and Meredith grappled in their pocketbooks for theirs. Samuel went to his study for his.

Lorraine retrieved hers slowly, watching the actions of those around her.

I'd lost all track of mine. "Can I get anyone anything?"

"Not for me, dear," said Nell.

"Thanks, I'm fine," said Jim.

"Wow," Lorraine said, "I'd always thought of this as a party. What is this other?"

"A lot of fun," said Charles.

"A grand old time," said Old Sarah.

"Supper some Saturday night," said Samuel, as he returned. "We'll eat outside if the weather allows."

"Are you sure you don't want us to bring anything?" said Lorraine, watching Samuel sit again in his recliner.

"There's no need of that, Mrs. Davis," he said. "Everyone can bring his or herself, and that will be quite enough for you to do."

"You can bring Mike if you want," I said to her.

For the first time in all the times Lorraine had been in my presence, the ghost of pain flickered in her eyes.

She'd never mentioned her husband, I realized. She never spoke of him at all.

"Why, thank you," said Lorraine. "I'll be sure and ask him."

I ought to have been delirious with victory, but I was not easy now. I didn't know exactly what I had just uncovered.

"Let's plan this," said Old Sarah. "What riches for us."

All of us together set a date for the party, a Friday night— since, it turned out, no Saturday would work—in late June.

///// //// ///// // ////////

This is the word the Lord God gives, and I write it as it comes.

Their laughter topples me at the knees. I am buried by the avalanche of mountainside. Veins shatter like glass.

I spill like water and like blood, and the ground soaks me into it.

My own child loves her best. Better than me.

If I am true, I would, too.

Surely this book will prove to the tenure review committee what Lorraine is about. I will have to work fast to keep her from fabricating my failings to them before I have a chance to finish.

God, I am losing. I am losing. I live in a world of fear, when I used to be so brave.

I have to fight what is happening.

My life will be destroyed if I don't.

Dr. Rickwell will never have me on her wall.

Some conspiracy goes on, nefarious and appalling. Out of the corners of my eyes, I see.

It terrifies me—enrages—how much care Samuel seems to take with her.

///// //// ////// // ////////

*T*he snarling wildness came over me on the way home with Ian.

I could not find a way to ease it.

Which unsettled me even more.

Meredith was sick and had been all week. Samuel's docket that week was exceptionally full.

"You two take care of your supper," he'd said when I called around noon to say Meredith wouldn't be at the house, "and I'll fend for myself when I get there. That will be simplest. And help you manage best, I think."

I did not disagree.

I was cutting in and out of traffic. Slow always pissed me off, but now it made me livid. I wanted to lop everyone's heads off, leave spouting bloody stumps behind for necks. I wanted to get us home.

"Scoot," Ian said, or maybe it was, "Shoot."

"Hang on, baby." I despised fast food. I would make us sandwiches, and we were going to make it, we were going to survive.

I brought Ian's highchair into the kitchen and sat him in it. I gave him Giant, and I gave him the scrupulously mended Lammykin. "Mommy's making supper," I said. "You can play here a minute."

I started pulling ingredients from the refrigerator. Ian began to bang on the tray.

When I turned, he grinned at me. "Lamm-y-kin-walk." He banged with the flat of his hand to mark each syllable.

I could feel anger revving up my bloodstream. "Could Lammykin walk softer, please?"

Ian smacked the tray once. "Please?"

I wanted to slip off my skin and peel the nerves away. "What if I made you toast and honey?" As much as I hated bribing my son, especially with food when I was getting dinner, if he focused on eating, maybe he would settle down, and I could get things together—myself included—without killing us both.

(These thoughts were, of course, not thoughts, defined, plodding, methodical. They were forged of white-hot impulse.)

Ian lifted his hands and opened his arms. "Me honey."

So I toasted bread and cut it in pieces. I buttered and honeyed them and set them before my awed and quietened son. "There." I rounded back to my earlier preparations. Ian was humming and mumbling, and the banging had stopped.

Soon enough I had one cheese sandwich and one turkey sandwich, plus green pepper strips and apple slices, ready to go. "Okay, buddy," I said to Ian at my back, "let's get you set up in the other room."

I crossed to the highchair and—the child in it was covered in honey.

His hands. His face, his hair. His shirt. His toys.

Satisfaction was evident in the shine of his eyes, the set of his mouth.

I was electrocuted with mad. My body crackled, and my brain roasted.

I had cleaned up many a honey mess before now. After all, this was my son, the honey lover. But I could not remember any moment but this one, the one in which I was enraged.

"Goddamn you little son of a bitch!" I jerked the tray off the highchair and pitched it on the floor.

The look on his face should have connected with me. It could not reach me.

I seized Ian and yanked him out. He blubbered. He screamed. I hauled him upstairs, and he wailed and flailed.

I hollered, "Stop it! I want you to stop! I just want to get the fucking dinner done!" My eyes traveled along with us but never sent anything coherent to my brain, because my brain was burning up. My head was torched by anger, because I had to deal with the annoyance of cleaning him.

In the bathroom, I slung a washcloth out of the cabinet and dumped Ian at the sink. I was yelling words, strings of words as I tugged off his shirt. He was shrieking and bawling and begging. I remember noise, and I remember blurs as we moved. I could not see my son for the boiling wrath. I could not hear him. He scarcely registered.

I had the wet washcloth in my hand and was scrubbing him vigorously, my other arm tight around him, and Ian and I were both as loud as we could make ourselves. Another voice roared out, and I was seized, and Ian was wrenched away, I don't know how, it was all at once.

Then I was let go. The washcloth sloshed from my hand to the floor.

Even looking at Samuel, I barely understood where any of us were. Fury overloaded me still.

"I don't know what this is," my husband said, every word forceful yet controlled, "what you think you're doing here. But it is clear to me that you'd damn well better get yourself figured out."

Ian howled and clung to Samuel. Beneath the towering rage, I found an eerie hollowness.

"I think I need to lie down," I said.

Samuel gave a curt, perfunctory gesture with his head. "You go do that."

I emptied myself from the room, listening to Ian weep.

I went to the bedroom, but it was like I had left the house entirely. The place was full of shadows. The roil of my mind continued, farther and farther from where I was. I stretched myself out on the bed, my arms reaching for nothing. I was shaking. I was slowly draining away.

////// //// ////// // ////////

My Five-Times Plea—June 2005
(Variations on the Following Theme):

"Hello? Yes, hi. This is Susan again? Yes, I called a few days ago and left a message for the pastor to call me, please—do you know if he got the message?

"Yes, ma'am, I'm sure you did, I just—I need to talk to him. I'm not a member there, but I've been attending, and I am planning to join.

"Well, it's of an urgent nature, something is scary wrong with me, and I don't know, but it frightens me. I've prayed about it—I believe in God, I really do—but right now, I just don't understand why God's not seeming to listen. That's what I want to speak with the pastor about.

"Yes, ma'am, I'm sure he's very busy. It's a huge church, I understand. But I'm a little new at all this, and I could use the help. I mean, I would've thought God would be helping me if I'm sincere and praying, but I can't tell that anything's changing, so that part's a little worrisome, too.

"Please, yes, if you could take my number down again, and my name, and just explain that I'm mixed-up and I'm struggling and something is very wrong, and ask him if he can get back with me as soon as he can. I'd be extremely grateful if he could meet with me and talk with me.

"Okay, yes, thank you. Yes, that's it. Thank you very much. Okay. Goodbye."

///// //// ////// // ////////

That Friday in late June, I was bedecked in my new teal dress and shoes and necklace to match. I looked like a prom queen. I'd tried to read some in the new Bible study book, but could not concentrate enough—I could only skim the first paragraph again and again.

But that morning I'd had energy, and I'd had optimism, and I still retained some measure of both, and the evening was set to turn lush and hot, the perfect night for our party.

All my misgivings had been erased from my mind as if they'd never been.

Except, of course, for Lorraine.

The daylilies were dying in their vase.

In the magnificent light and lengthening shadows of the summer's evening, Jim and Nell, Nate and Charles, Old Sarah and Meredith, and Ian and I waited outdoors among the tablecloth-spread tables.

First we waited (actually, Meredith, Ian, and I had waited) for the potato salad and pasta salad, the coleslaw and fruit salad, until the caterers delivered it all on time. The brownies were iced and had chocolate sprinkles and powdered sugar on them.

(Ian periodically bounced and cavorted before the table where the brownie tray was set. "Yummy cookie," he said. I told him there was supper first.)

Then we waited on the chancellor and the banjo player.

We waited fifteen minutes. Twenty. We drank beer and diet soda, lemonade and water.

I checked my phone. I checked the house phone. I called Samuel's phone, and it went straight to voice mail. "Hello," I said, "just calling to see if you're on your way home, hope nothing's the matter. Please let me hear, love you."

I didn't have a telephone number for Lorraine.

No one else did either.

"I guess something came up that he needed to finish," I said. "I'm sorry we're late getting started."

But Samuel always called. Always.

"My doctor's office left a message for me once," said Nell, "and it didn't show up on my cell phone for two days."

But I saw the sad, tentative look in her eyes.

"I called Nate this one time, and his phone never rang," said Charles. "No missed call, nothing. Like it never happened."

"That's technology for you," said Old Sarah, chuckling.

The longer we waited, the more certain I became of the reason for the delay. My mouth was very dry.

"Mommy? Cookie? Cookie, Mommy?" said Ian.

I caved and let him have a brownie.

When half an hour had gone by, I turned to Jim. "I'm getting the meat," I said. "We're going ahead."

"You're sure?"

"Yes. There's no reason for us all to go hungry." I felt wilted and absurd in my new clothes.

Meredith and I brought out the meat, and Jim set to work.

"Please, come on, you all," I said, once he'd gotten things underway. "Get yourselves a plate."

We were queued up, serving ourselves the sides, then heading to Jim for our steak or chicken, when Lorraine and Samuel entered the back yard from the house.

"Susan," said Samuel, "I was going to help Jim with the grill, I said we were coming."

"When?" I said. "When did you say that?"

"In the message I left, about thirty-five, forty minutes ago."

I looked at my phone. I saw the message. (Had I missed it? How had I missed it?) "It's here now. Did you get mine?"

"Of course."

The others did not move. Were watching us.

"I had no message," I said. None of this made sense. Samuel would have told us to go ahead and eat. He would hate to keep our friends waiting. "Ian was hungry and so were the rest of us, and I didn't have the faintest idea where you were."

"I'm so sorry, Susan," said Lorraine, "I was rear-ended at a red light. And my car was knocked into the car ahead of me."

After all that God had shown me, I couldn't believe that this was the truth.

"My goodness," said Nell. "Were you hurt?"

"I don't think so, not too bad. I'll probably be sore tomorrow. But my car's in pretty rough shape." Lorraine brandished her hands while she talked. "I was waiting for the police to arrive, calling my insurance company, calling a rollback. And Chancellor Ellison came by. He stopped and waited there with me until the tow guy came. It was very kind."

A sort of bursting in my brain rocketed pieces of me apart like fireworks, and everything I wanted to say started coming out of my mouth. "What kind of ridiculous story is that?"

I was looking at Samuel, not Lorraine, which surprised even me. I could feel that everyone there was watching me.

"What would have been ridiculous," said Samuel, "was to drive on and leave her there. Since she was coming here, too."

"I know what she's doing. I know what she's been up to. I know everything. And so do you apparently."

"You know, Susan, just now, you don't sound very lucid at all to me."

"That's because you don't believe how I do. You haven't seen what I've seen."

Samuel's brow descended. "I think we ought to continue this later."

"Fine. Everyone is going to know soon enough. I'm going to put it in my book."

Ian made a quavering sound. Meredith was holding onto him.

I shouldn't have mentioned the book. The truth would disturb many.

"Write all you please," said Samuel, "but it's going to be a pretty damn slim volume if that's your objective, to expose some crime of mine against you. If you were anything like yourself, you'd know that."

Ian gave a sharp shriek. Meredith brought her head nearer like she whispered to him. I wanted to protect him from my words, but also I had to say what I hadn't said, what needed to be said now.

"I *am* myself. Why wouldn't I be?"

Samuel took one swift step toward me. "That's the same fucking question I'm asking here." And he turned away.

All my breath had been wrenched from me.

This was the tipping point where I now lived. My body flooded with an immersion of enormous cold as I realized how I'd struggled to stay balanced there.

I couldn't name what was the matter. But it had to start mattering. Even if underneath I was still me. I saw that now.

Nell was looking at me, and, as though I were her, I could see myself in that moment. In that tinge of sorrow.

II
SUSAN

(SECOND SUSAN)

Annika Johnson wrote on a large legal pad, her back to her desk, her chair turned to me. She wore her hair in a long, dark braid, and her embroidered peasant blouse and dark slacks made a distinctive choice of uniform. Her body was quiet.

I envied her economy of motion, her self-containment.

I coveted such evident wholeness.

The pictures on the walls of her office—I supposed it was right to call the room that—were varied and colorful.

A house stitched of rainbow thread.

A stylized colored-pencil sketch of children holding hands like paper dolls in an unbroken chain.

Quilted mountains purpling into some forever distance.

I supposed her breezy art was intended to put me at ease. It didn't. I felt estranged from it, from every good feeling it was meant to evoke.

Only one photo was there, on the woman's desk, of an assemblage of adults and children and a cockatoo in their midst that I took to be her family.

We seemed near in age, Annika and I.

"So," she said, "Dr. Huffman? Susan? What is it you want to talk to me about today?"

A week earlier, I'd met Nell for lunch. "Nell," I'd been ready to say, "please give me your friend's name and phone number," but she'd thrust the business card at me even before she sat at the table. I'd zipped it into my wallet, stuffed the wallet into my bag.

"I want to talk," I said to Annika, "about why I'm degenerating into this unholy mess."

"Can you describe for me what's going on?" she said.

Therapists, in every fictional portrayal or representation I'd ever seen, had couches for their clients to lie back on. Annika had only a chair for me. It was not an unlikable chair.

I thought of myself as a client. Not a patient. That's how I was coping.

"Maybe," I said. I had no trouble speaking to a roomful of students, but I had reservations about speaking to her. What I had to say was so very private.

But then I'd come there to obtain her expertise. And to bring that about, I'd have to talk.

So I did. I confessed how hard it could be to get out of bed some mornings. How I struggled to stay invested in my job when I once cared for it deeply. How I had trouble maintaining patience with Ian, and how Samuel did not sympathize with my newfound faith.

I did omit my conviction that Samuel and Lorraine were seeing each other. Annika Johnson was a stranger to me, and my husband's livelihood depended upon the public's perception of his scrupulous life.

Neither did I mention the vision I'd had in my study, since that was a deeply personal event and not a symptom of anything that I could see.

Annika wrote on her legal pad as she listened. This made me nervous.

When I told her all that seemed right to tell, I finished by asking, "Is now when you ask me to talk about my mom and my dad and all that?" I was not looking forward to sharing this.

"You can talk about them if you want to," she said, "but our main focus in here would be on your thoughts and your behavior. The goal is to help you begin to choose ways of thinking and patterns of action that are helpful to your life rather than otherwise."

I was surprised by her response. "Maybe that would be of some kind of help later on," I said, "but my main focus here right now is to put a name to whatever is wrong with me."

"I'm a social worker. I can't diagnose you. But I can most definitely help you, if you're willing."

"I'm skeptical, frankly."

"That's okay. That's an okay place to start from."

I was not sure how to take Annika Johnson, LCSW. Her expression both calculating and compassionate.

"Can you tell me," she said, "when you first thought you were having difficulty?"

"Two or three months ago. I got bent out of shape over a toy of my son's." I mumbled this quickly, embarrassed and ashamed. But God had been warning me of difficulty in my life, I realized, for some time before that. Since Lorraine's intrusion. "I don't know, though, maybe it's been going on for longer."

"Have there been any changes in your life? Anything you can pinpoint?"

I put my hands in my lap, arranged my thoughts. "I'm starting the process of going up for tenure in the fall. At first I thought that was what was different—the pressure of knowing what's coming, I mean—and I'd just ride things out. But the whole situation in my life has gotten so very ugly. Before that I had a—religious experience. That caused a degree of change for me, too."

Annika had been writing. She stopped, lifted her head.

"If you can't diagnose me," I said, "where do I go so that can happen?"

Whatever she thought of all I'd said, she still wore the kindly, clinical look on her face, the way she wore her braid, the embroidered blouse. As an interesting choice of uniform. "That's what a psychiatrist would do."

I did not much like the sound of her words. They crashed like planes against my eardrums, went up in flames in my mind. "All right."

"You can come back when you want. It doesn't matter when. You're established here now."

The fires burned higher. "We'll see," I was able to say. I did not trust myself to nod, to acquiesce to the corridors that seemed to be shutting in, smothering me with their disorienting, hideous mirrors, the ghastly appearance of my face in them, wherever I turned. Annika's carefully cheery office was apparently just the start of this lurid ride, which I could not seem to exit.

///// //// ///// // ////////

The house was always quiet now. It tossed and sighed with white noise. Fan blades gyred, whirled their dance up at the ceiling.

It comforted me and troubled me together.

Samuel removed to Joel's old room. "I'm giving you some space," he said.

In return, I could hardly find a feeling in myself. I was too full. I was too empty.

I stayed in the bedroom as much as possible. Meredith came often.

Below my floor, people entered the rooms of our house, mumbled things, brought meals to the family as though I'd died. Great continents of time drifted between their arrivals.

I read from the Psalms when I was able. When I could not, with both arms I gripped my Bible against me where I lay curled on my side. I was mystified by my behavior. It came out of me, and there was nothing else for me to do.

A few times Nell braved the stairs, peered into the room, and spoke to me. Overcome by her human voice, I answered in what whispered tatters I could muster.

It was hard to be seen. It was hard to let a friend into this place of suffering.

Lorraine visited me once.

"Susan?"

I recognized the voice, and I rolled, I sat up from the sheets to see how this woman dared bring herself to the door of my room.

Lorraine wore an expression that said she was carrying some luminous secret to share, and she had what looked to be a parfait glass in her hand. "I brought supper for you all, I hope you don't mind, but this dessert is for you."

"Why would I mind?" I slung my question like a javelin at her. I wondered how many suppers she had brought, how many times she had delivered her consoling presence to my family, fed my husband.

"Because." She stood so quietly that she might have been only a shadow, cast there by some immovable fixture. "You don't care much for me. I don't know why."

I sank against the headboard. "Lorraine, that's not true." I did not want to have this conversation, most certainly not now.

"No. You're not being kind at all, though maybe you think you are." She was a voice coming from the corners of the room. She edged closer. "Your lie is much crueler than the truth. It means you think I'm too simple to know that you've accused me." I could see the sheen of her eyes.

I wanted to scream at her, to call her all the names there were, to snatch up and hurl the parfait glass so it would shatter in her face. I did not have the strength. I should not tire myself that way. "I don't know why I said those things at the party. I haven't been right, I've been off for some time. That doesn't excuse anything, I know."

She stopped, halfway into the room. "I've only wanted us to be friends." A tremor rippled through her voice, a helpless drop and surge. "I wish I knew what I wanted in my life the way you do."

I was afraid of everything she said and wondered if I lay down and turned my face to the wall then she would leave. This encounter reminded me of my mother, speaking a prayer over my bed to me out of the night, when I'd roused, surfaced, then drowsed beneath the sound of her words. I did not want this moment with Lorraine to remind me of my mother. I would not know what to do with my very clear warnings from God if Lorraine were sincere.

The fan murmured overhead. "I'm so sorry this has happened, Susan. I hope you can find out what's wrong." Lorraine walked toward the bed again. I caught the wink of the glass.

"It's good of you to come and help out my family." I closed my eyes with the weariness of it all.

"You have the most beautiful life together, you and Chancellor Ellison." She smelled of the wind. "You don't know how fortunate you are, and how much that's given me courage and hope, too, in my own circumstances."

My eyes came open. There she was, so honest and humble and ordinary, so perfectly irreproachable. I couldn't conceive how any circumstances of hers could be other than bounteous. No one could be insensible to her appeal, though I wanted to be, and it stunned me that she could not know this of herself.

She reached the bed and offered the food to me. In that moment, I believed her. Deeply. Without reservation.

////// //// ////// // ////////

I'm lying in bed. Turned on my side, my face to the wall.

Heavy curtains are shut against the afternoon sun on a Monday in early July.

Beside me in bed sprawls a thick book, a provider directory, opened to the listing of psychiatrists that will accept my insurance.

Beside me also is my sleek touchtone telephone, dragged from the nightstand to be within reach so I can dial numbers on it.

In the last hour I have called number after number. With great spaces between.

None of the psychiatrists I've called are accepting new patients.

I understand that I have to keep calling.

I understand that I am running out of options.

To move my hand is to stretch it the distance of a thousand miles.

To move my hand is for my whole body to trudge that distance.

I'm lying in bed. Looking at the phone. Seeing the book.

It is as though I have been locked in chains.

In commercials on television, they make this seem so simple. Call a number for help. And, there you have friendly, soothing voices. Instant help. You are safe.

I've seen it a thousand times.

They never show the scenario where no doctor will see you, treat you, talk to you. They never show the consequences of that reality.

What it looks like when you're your own help, when you should not be, when you can't be at all.

Here I am. On my side.

There is the phone.

There is my hand.

I can't move.

I can't move.

I can't.

With enormous effort, my hand crosses to the farthest coast, reaches, fumbles, grasps the receiver.

I can't say why. Why my mind won't work and then it did.

I only know the act is momentous.

I dial the phone again.

///// //// ///// // ///////

I went to see the doctor. The only psychiatrist who could see me.

The doctor listened to me, asked me things. Then sent me for a psychological evaluation.

I guessed he wanted to do this right.

I wanted him to, I guessed.

The day of the evaluation was cold for July. All the surfaces in the world trailed fog into the air in slender tendrils which appeared like souls. All the world's surfaces were so damp they might never be dry. They were so chilled they might never be warm.

I entered a gray building and a subterranean room. The fluorescent lights hummed their pink-tinged, ghastly sheen down the walls, the carpeting, the furniture, until I thought I would be pressed to my death in it.

At a table, I sat with a man whose name I have lost. We seemed alone in the building, the evaluator and I. We'd become the only people in existence.

I spent the morning taking test after test after test. I listened to the scroll of the pen, the whisper of papers.

I'd always been an excellent test-taker. I'd always expected excellent results. I could not imagine what these answers were going to reveal.

But, damn it, I was going to answer everything as thoroughly as possible.

I wanted to know.

I wanted to know.

Though I kept my jacket on in that place of ice, the unnatural light seeped into me just the same.

When the psychiatrist saw me again several days later—on a seasonably blistering summer afternoon—he had my results in hand, and he proposed his answer to me.

I had worn my black Kaspar interview suit. As though it might protect me somehow. Which, of course, was ridiculous.

I had prayed for days. Which I believed could truly help.

"There's a lot of information here, Susan," he said. "Perhaps you'd want to discuss some of it with your therapist, and our office can release a copy to her. But what seems most relevant in your responses, especially given your earlier description of your problem, leads me to a diagnosis of bipolar disorder."

I frowned. I tried to summon what I knew about those words. It was vaguely disturbing. And I should probably be alarmed. Bipolar was a thing I had seen on TV. In the eyes of actors playing stalkers and workplace shooters. I was trying to comprehend the connection between them and me.

The doctor was writing on a prescription pad. "I'm taking you off the antidepressant. It's going to be very important that you take your new medication every day. Exactly as prescribed."

I nodded. "Of course." I could barely absorb what was happening, the doctor tearing the paper from the pad, my own fingers reaching out to grasp it.

I could tell only that I had dipped the nail of my little toe into the shadowed enormity of what stretched ahead.

Leaving the doctor's office, I stumbled out the door into a white-hot brightness. The sun had bleached the sky and everything underneath it with a shattering light. After the dimness of the interior, I could not find anything, not even my own hand. Squinting, blinking, staggering, I searched the parking lot for some sign of my car. My head did not pertain to me. It had been severed from my shoulders and rolled away. A feeling foreign to me.

I supposed I would get accustomed. I would have to learn to get by.

///// //// ////// // ////////

Samuel came home.

All afternoon, I had wondered what to say. I'd changed out of my suit into the most uncomplicated dress I owned—so it would not exhaust me to wear it—a pale pink knit that pulled over my head. I'd helped Meredith with supper as much as possible, setting the table, working the blender for the gazpacho. I wanted to convey a confidence and a relief I did not feel.

When Samuel saw me, the look of his eyes pinched. His face remained impassive. "Well, you look better."

I knew there was nothing much to say until Meredith left.

I limped a smile. "It isn't easy."

"I don't think it is," he said.

At supper, Samuel ate half of what was on his plate. We didn't speak of his day or mine, mention the vacation we had concluded we shouldn't take. Ian fussed and whined in his highchair until I collected him, let his weight settle against me and onto me.

"Me done," he said.

I wasn't hungry either.

Afterward, I helped Meredith put my son to bed. To do this, I walked past the door to my study twice. There it stood, without me. Neglected. And I was ashamed. It was not mine now, and I did not know when it would be mine again.

Samuel sat in the living room in his recliner, unreclined, looking at an open book.

Meredith left. The front door bumped, and the room grew large.

I stood in the midst of it, the primary focal point.

I sank to the couch.

Samuel's book was already shut. "What was the doctor's opinion?"

This was going to be a conversation of blurts, I supposed. "That I'm bipolar."

A jolt vanished across his face. "I'm sorry."

The whir of fan blades. The bland gray of the carpet. The sickly gray.

"I don't even know what that means, really. I'm going to find out."

"I expect that you will."

His tone was different from what I'd meant. I heard him as a bass drum of doom. But I had to plow on as though I hadn't. "It's just, I don't know how long it will take."

"Of course you don't. It's impossible to say."

I'd been leaning forward, my hands pressed together in my lap. I sat back against the cushions. "What do you want me to say?"

"It might be better for you to consider what you are going to *do.*"

The room was falling in. "What do you mean? I'm going to get my sanity back, Samuel."

My husband had considered the cases of many, many people whose sanity was compromised, whose liberty might need to be constrained for the safety of others and for their own sake. He looked at me carefully. "Maybe," he said.

////// //// ////// // ////////

At the height of summer, I inhabited a dark house. My son and Meredith rustled in some of the rooms by day.

But I was alone.

My pillow stank of sweat and staleness.

The pastor didn't call me back. He didn't call and didn't call.

His absence of acknowledgment began to feel like shunning. Like abandonment. The nothing I received was inexplicable.

Since he had no time to help me sort out my health and my faith, I turned the thin, crinkly pages of my Bible, desperate for comfort and counsel.

The story of a man healed from demon possession encouraged me at first, but it ended with the man restored to his sanity, untouched by illness for all time.

That was not going to happen to me here.

I looked for a biblical figure I could learn from, whose story resonated with mine, who had successfully lived out a damaged existence while still in communion with God.

I couldn't find one.

The type stuck to the page and did not enter me.

The drone of the fan fell over me, covered me like a blanket.

Maybe the pastor would return my calls if I were a member of his church. I wasn't a real, true member, only some anonymous visitor.

The drone of the fan warmed my body.

But I didn't see how I could fulfill any requirements of a membership process. I could not shower. I could not walk into my study.

My insides were ice.

If somehow I could enter my study, where I'd first seen the vision, then the remembrance would sustain me, and I would be in the presence of God.

I dragged the sheet over my face. If I could enter my study, where I'd first beheld the hope that I could *declare new ways*, I would experience an empty room with a gigantic hole in the air where my vision once was.

I began to think I was going to end like this, my head and limbs sinking with a weight greater than all the seas, my body all but motionless in a bed in a room in a house in a life in a marriage that once was joyously mine and freely welcomed me.

I was silent. I was screaming, and there was no one to hear.

////// //// ////// // ////////

"**D**r. Huffman?" Dr. Rickwell looked so very sad to see me as I entered her office.

"Thank you for meeting with me," I said.

That morning, I'd hauled myself out of bed. It had taken all my willpower to get under the shower. For so many reasons.

I'd put my clothing on one agonizing piece after another.

Making up my face was beyond me.

Nell drove me to campus. She waited in the car. Samuel could not get away.

I'd been on medication for a week. I was dizzy, discombobulated, still unaccustomed to the medicine.

Ian was home with Meredith.

Fall semester would start in less than a month.

I had a meeting I could not miss.

Dr. Rickwell gestured toward the chair in front of her desk. "I'm so sorry to see you under these circumstances. You say a health concern has come up?"

"Yes." I put myself into the chair before I ended up in the floor. "I wanted to let you know at the earliest possible moment and discuss the situation with you in person, if I could at all."

My face was scorching, blistering in the stares from all her photographs. I couldn't look at the brave she-roes. I wished every one of them faced the wall.

"What would I need to do," I said, "to request a leave of absence? And permission to delay my tenure review?"

Dr. Rickwell examined me. "This is very serious." She spoke as if she had difficulty believing what I'd just said.

"I understand it to be."

She exhaled a long and controlled breath. "Dr. Huffman, I hate to hear this. I truly do."

"So do I." During the semester I'd given birth to Ian, my teaching load had been redistributed among my colleagues, but

I'd continued my other work from home. I was a nine-month employee. There was no FMLA choice for me.

Dr. Rickwell swiveled her chair back and forth, stopped. "To make your request, you'd need to discuss it with the department head. And that's precisely the kind of situation I'm here as your mentor for, to help you facilitate that."

I could feel how much easier my breath filled my body. "Thank you, Dr. Rickwell."

A curious look came over her face. "I must say, I'd wondered about you at the end of last semester. You seemed more—scattered to me. I know Dr. Mackey had voiced some frustration."

"Yes. I'm afraid so." I didn't have a clear memory of my meeting with Dr. Rickwell towards the end of the term. It seemed hazed and disassociated from me when I brought it to mind. "I'm sorry for the trouble and concern I've caused—and the inconvenience that I know this will cause. It has not been a good time." Had she mentioned Hugh's complaints to me then? Poor Hugh. I owed him an explanation.

"No, I'd say not. I know this has been a hard decision for you to make. I know how determined and dedicated you are."

I did not trust myself to speak. My throat was slick with bitterness.

"Dr. Huffman—Susan—" Dr. Rickwell leaned toward me "—you understand—your request can be risky. Not in all cases—" she added with a rush "—it depends on the candidate, the whole person and what she can bring to the position. But I would be remiss if I didn't say this to you."

My body continued to sit. My heart had crashed through the floor. That she would even voice the possibility of detriment was not a good sign. Since she would surely know I'd divined it already.

All my dreams of a book about Anna Maria Magdalena Muller, to teach the world about the extraordinary life of an Appalachian woman

All the years of sharing the riches of East Tennessee history with young people, to show them where they came from and directions they might go

All the stimulating work and discourse with colleagues who dreamed of furthering historical knowledge to help humanity shape a better future

All of this—everything I had been, everything I'd worked for, had hoped for—was falling away from me. Was being torn away. Because of this bipolar, a situation I could not control.

I swallowed and nodded. "It would be even less fair to my colleagues if I came back before I was fully able. And I think a leave of absence is the best way to get myself ready to come back."

She nodded slowly. Her face full of regret.

"Because I mean to come back," I said, "as dedicated to my work as I was before this started."

"Of course you do. And I want to have you here."

I felt like I had no face. Like I was disappearing before her eyes. I liked Dr. Rickwell. She deserved some gesture of thanks. I quirked the corners of my mouth out of gratitude and politeness. There was no way to make a smile.

"One other thing," she said. "You'll need to think about what you want to say to the department head. You're under no obligation to reveal the whole situation, obviously, but you'll need to decide what to tell him to have your request carefully considered."

I had suspected as much, had revolved that quandary already before I arrived.

It would all come down to this:

If I said too little, my request would not be granted.

Or, equally bad, it would be, but I would be marked as irresponsible, unable to cope with academic life.

If I said too much, I could be damaged irreparably as well.

When I came up for review, I was in trouble either way.

///// //// ///// // ///////

*I*nto the room where I huddled in my bed, Meredith carried Ian one morning. He was squirming and crying and importuning through a mouth full of water, "Mommy. Want Mommy."

I heaved myself up, and she put him in the bed next to me.

My poor son should have had a better mother.

Ian scrambled, and the bed wallowed. He lunged at me.

I hugged him tight, so tight. My child.

"Sick? Mommy sick?"

Meredith stayed to take him from me again.

"Just a little, sweetie. It's okay."

Ian burrowed himself against me, into me. "Better Mommy?"

"Mommy's going to be," I said. "Soon."

///// //// ///// // ///////

From the date my condition had a name, I became a student of my diagnosis. Of my illness.

The same way I had been a student of Tennessee history, of Anna Maria Magdalena Muller and the world in which she lived.

The same way I'd been a student of faith.

I dragged myself as much as I could stand it to the bookstore and to the library. Many, many books went home with me.

I wanted to know what my illness *was*. What having it would mean. I was not afraid to discover what those books would say.

I read:

Bipolar disorder was a chemical imbalance in my brain.

The medication I was prescribed was to try to regulate the imbalance, but the condition would never go away.

Along with medicine, the best treatment involved regulating and ordering the whole of my life. Therapy would teach me to tell when symptoms manifested and how to respond when they did. I needed to observe regular sleeping and waking hours, too, and manage the amount of stress I let into my life.

From now on, my first objective would be to keep the unpredictable flare-ups of irritation or crushing sadness, of anger or euphoria, from becoming wholly incendiary.

I found out antidepressants could actually exacerbate illness in people with bipolar disorder.

(The psychiatrist had taken me off my antidepressant, I recalled.)

The consequences if I did not take my medicine would be that my illness would worsen, and I would continue to have difficulty coping, and I would never hope to regain any semblance of normalcy in my life.

Many people with bipolar disorder did not take their medicine, believing themselves to be quite well, or they stopped taking it once the worst symptoms subsided.

Of course, if I did take my medicine, I would probably gain weight and face other substantial side effects as well.

And taking it didn't guarantee that my illness wouldn't worsen.

The books I consulted also suggested that it was helpful to keep a diary of my moods so I could objectively chart mood highs and lows and better communicate that information to my doctor at appointments.

I began notating my mood entries in the same book God had asked me to write. As I wrote, I prayed over my symptoms and asked for insight as I sought to understand what foreign invader had parachuted into my head.

It was terrifying, this process of relearning myself.

For the whole of my existence, I had always relied on my mind. I believed that it led me to the truth when I used it.

If the thoughts in my head were not reliable after all—if I was overrun by thoughts that were distinct and different from me—then where was I, who was I?

Since my thoughts could not be trusted, it seemed, I didn't stand much chance of ever knowing.

Like the dutiful pupil I was, I took the medicine as I was supposed to do. I was too much of a nerd not to obey my doctor. And I began gaining weight.

And, though the days and I seemed part of one seamless sameness, I began to emerge from that desolate territory and into myself once more.

////// //// ////// // ////////

"Mommy?" Ian hopped to me where I sat in the living room reading, repatriating myself to the house. He waved one of his shoes at the page and my face. "Me shoe, please?"

I slipped my head back a bit. "Careful there. Did it come off?" I could commiserate again. I laid the book beside me. "Want to get up here?"

He'd resisted my help with feeding and dressing often enough, hadn't wanted to wear shoes in the house. Until now.

"Yep," he said. He clambered as I reached, and I hoisted him into my lap. He had the shoe in one hand and Lammykin in the other. I coaxed the shoe away.

The marigolds were sharply bright in the back yard. Meredith was in the kitchen, getting supper ready.

Ian fidgeted. "Mommy make skyscrapers? Me make and Lammykin?" He arched and twisted his body to look back at me. He hadn't strayed far all day. He'd built blocks in the living room, latched himself to my thigh when we went to the dining room for lunch.

"I don't know. We'll see." I'd gotten the shoe onto his foot and began working with the laces.

Ian gave me a stern look. "Mommy better." He jerked his head with each word as he made his emphatic pronouncement.

Before I could puzzle out if I'd received an affirmation regarding the state of my health or a threat, I heard the opening of the door from the garage into the kitchen.

That was Samuel.

"I bet Daddy's home," I said to Ian.

It had been too long since my son was settled against me and I'd been able to bear his weight. Only now could I stand to be in the same room with people without feeling that my skin was being shaved off my bones.

I caught fragments of conversation, and Samuel emerged from the kitchen.

"Hi, Daddy." Ian eagerly opened and closed fingers at his father.

Samuel did not answer, focused straight on me. "Is that a situation you can handle there?"

The situation was: Ian sitting in my lap.

With his toy. And shoes on both feet.

"Yes," I said.

There was a shiver near my heart.

A suggestion of accusation.

"Very good." Samuel headed to his study to shed his briefcase. "Hello, Ian."

I let Ian slide to the floor. Inside of my husband's question I detected another.

Was I—or was I not—safe enough to care for my son?

///// //// ///// // ///////

Okay, God. You gave this book to me. You told me to write about Lorraine so I'd see what was to come, rising from the pages and pointing a spectral finger where I should look.

But this I did not see coming.

Did you?

Tell me.

If you can talk at all, tell me.

And while you are at it, explain to me

Why

///// //// ///// // ///////

I did not want to enter my church.

So I drove to the Catholic hospital in Edenton.

Ian was with me. I carried him down antiseptic hallways into the chapel.

An extravagant, ethereal room filled with haunting shapes.

The room was the color of wood and of gold. The floors were marble.

My feet sent out echoes of our presence.

We harbored in the dim and quiet pew.

Before us stood Jesus with his burning heart and one hand outstretched as though about to bestow some great miracle—in the very next moment, perhaps—but not yet, not just yet.

I wondered when it would finally come.

Ian pointed. "He got Lammykin, too."

A sheep lay across Christ's shoulders.

"Yes." I wondered if this detail was some sign of divine reproach. I still handled my own son's toy with revulsion. Every time I touched it.

Jesus looked so beautiful I wanted to cry.

"Mommy?" Ian sounded perplexed. "What he on fire?"

I shook my head. Jesus' heart looked fearsome and powerful, an image mysterious to me. "I don't know. He loves you a whole lot, it means, maybe."

"He know me's here?"

"He's supposed to." I was trying with all my might to hold to this belief. I maintained what I hoped was a posture of faith, my head lifted, my hands folded, my body attentive, reverent.

Christ looked as if he could stir at any moment. Step down to where we huddled. Speak to me, explain to me how I could declare new ways as an unemployed madwoman.

You came into my study. I never asked for you.

I trusted you.

Ian began to squirm. "It dark."

I *want to trust you, God. I want to love you now.*

I watched. I listened. Jesus stayed. Exactly as he was.

///// //// ///// // ////////

I stopped outside my husband's open study door. "Samuel?" Though he rarely shut his door when he was in working, I rarely approached him there. "I'm going up."

He nodded, looking at his desk, what was still to be done. "You have a difficult day ahead."

I was touched for him to say this, because he'd said so little to me of late, and because it was true. Tomorrow I was meeting with the head of the history department.

"Are you," I said, "coming soon?" He was still sleeping in the spare room. I was thinking of asking him back.

He moved some papers to the side, turned them over. "I doubt it."

His hand remained on the upside-down papers he had touched. His large, commanding hand. His sexy hand.

I said, "Are those philistines of yours causing you a lot of trouble tonight?"

I expected him to say, "Ah, yes. The philistines." I hoped for him to say that.

His shoulders jerked—the least twinge—and then he got very still.

"Susan," he said. "My God."

I must have stumbled into some particularly nasty case, joked of no joking matter. But before I could make amends, he looked at me from his tired face. His big hand still unmoved.

"It would," he said—his voice sardonic, recovered, yet slightly taut—"appear that way."

And he was correct. It did.

Reassured, I thought nothing more of my blunder that night.

///// //// ///// // ////////

And so I met with the department head.

(My perspiring palms on the steering wheel, beforehand, as I prayed in the parking lot.)

And I was granted a leave of absence.

I said that I'd been diagnosed with a serious illness, a mood disorder, and I needed to pursue a course of treatment before returning to work.

Telling that took all the fortitude I possessed.

Leaving the meeting, I knew that every word I'd said could be used against me upon my return.

If I ever returned.

/// //// ////// // ////////

It began as a good day, that Saturday in late August.

There had not been many of them for me for many weeks.

We'd eaten a late breakfast of Eggo waffles and pre-cooked, microwaved bacon.

Afterward, Ian and I sat on the couch and watched *Dumbo*. A difficult film to watch—the crows, the mother elephant, disturbed me. For different reasons.

But Ian snuggled with his hands on my arm and his head leaned into me, until I put both arms around him, and then he breathed against me, his chest reminding me over and over that he was there.

Samuel had lingered in the living room with us at first, reading, then disappeared into his study.

I tried to ignore my disappointment.

Later, with Ian down for his nap upstairs, I'd returned to the couch with a book in my lap and basked now in the sun of late summer. The living room curtains were opened, and it was a drowsy sort of afternoon. The rays penetrated my skin and lit my heart, stirring it toward germination. At last I could read with focus and savor the good feel of pages beneath my fingertips. I caressed the pages, smoothed them. I could still think. I could know the tantalization of others' ideas as they thronged into my mind.

"Susan?"

The book jounced, and I did, too.

Samuel was right there in the room with me, right in front of me.

He had approached without my knowing. A tall, big-framed man like he was.

So he had taken care to do it. Which was not at all usual.

And I detected reticence in that choice.

"Yes?" I scanned all the way up to his face, the one he'd brought out for me—well-ordered, considered, an official face—

But paired with searching eyes.

I was comprehending that pairing.

A trickle of cold, creeping terror began to fill me. Drown me.

"This will not continue," he said, "you and I.

"I'm filing to divorce you."

The book dropped away and struck the floor.

The force knocked me forward.

My hands covered my face.

"This is going to be what's best," he said.

"How? How is that best?" My diaphragm spasmed. I jerked my hands away and thrust up my head. "Good Lord, Samuel, I am sick. I'm sick, this is not my fault. You think I asked for this?"

"No. Of course not."

He sat beside me. The closest we had been in weeks, a mockery of proximity, and I twisted away, my hand to my mouth.

Now I understood the sight of his hand on those overturned papers.

"I want you to be well," he said, "I want to see you well, and I think you're going to be occupied with that for some time."

All I was occupied with in that moment was the knowledge that Samuel recognized what my childhood had been, how others had failed me, deliberately and otherwise, and yet he was choosing to do this to us.

He said, "It's going to take all your resources, I think, as you work towards health, and I think it will be better for us— certainly for you, as well as for Ian and me—if we continue with our separate lives."

But already I was scrambling, leaping up from the couch. I whirled about with my arms wrapped tight around me. "What do you mean *Ian*? You and *Ian*?"

Samuel regarded me with severe patience. "Susan. You've been unable to care for him in weeks. Before that, you were getting frustrated with him. Overly so. That is not a good situation."

"Good God, Samuel—" I opened my hands. "—Ian is my baby. I am his mother."

Samuel looked stung. "He's my son also. But, yes, he needs you. I realize that. As much as you are able to be with him and manage him."

It was remarkable how like my husband this man looked. My fists were at my sides. "You know I won't let this happen. Not without a fight."

"Did you think I would expect something different?" A touch of fervor—admiration? approval?—inside his voice, soon gone.

"I don't know. I don't know you." I was shaking my head. "You don't love me. You never loved me." I'd been rendered unrecognizable. An animal. A battered, bleeding body.

His eyes flickered with surprise. "That was never said."

I loved him, and I could choke on that, but that fact—that feeling—would make no difference.

This man was going to try to take my child from me, and I hated him.

"I'm going to Mamaw's and Papaw's."

"Don't be absurd. You can have the house."

"I don't want the fucking house."

A slow heaviness entered his face. "You detest it out there."

"Well," I said. "It's mine." I'd kept it these years—no doubt foolishly at times, although I'd thought it wise. Not because of sentiment—because it was something to have.

He looked at me. Delivered a curt nod. "I'll call the movers."

"Oh, Jesus." I shut my eyes.

"Yes, that would be good here. For everyone's sake."

My heart my breath the chanting of my mind

My baby my God my baby

My knees were going to drop me the first chance.

"Susan, I want you to understand," Samuel went on, "I don't want you worrying about your treatment. I'm prepared to do whatever's necessary in order for you to have what you need. I won't have you starve."

My eyes opened. As did my mouth, shocking me with what I said: "My life, Samuel, is not going to be about what you will or won't have. Not ever again."

He seemed stunned also. Bewildered. Angry.

"I know you aren't filing for divorce because of the space I need," I said. "Can you tell me what this is about?"

He produced a protracted breath. "There needs to be some harmony here. There needs to be some peace."

"Wouldn't that be nice? Only I'm not going to have any. None of us will, in fact."

"I know that, too."

I could not come apart here, not in front of him. He'd examined our lives already from every vantage point, arrived at his opinion, and there was nothing for me to say. Nothing. I turned to go upstairs.

And stumbled on the fallen library book.

Pitched forward one, two steps. Was righting myself.

The noise of movement behind me, Samuel rising from the couch. "Susan?" The shift in his voice as he stepped toward me.

I did not look. I had my balance. I thrust my arm back and lifted my middle finger. I went for the stairs.

In my room, I slammed the door and sank down behind it. My backbone against the wood. My knees up. Nothing could come in. I could think all the thoughts I wished, and outside, the sunshine was falling as before.

I had finally returned to my study. It would not be for long.

///// //// ///// // ///////

I was going to give God one more chance to help me.

I drove to my church on a weekday morning and headed for the church office. In my interview suit again.

The gray-headed secretary was typing on her computer.

"Hello," I said. "I've been trying to see the pastor. Is there any chance he's available today?"

The secretary, who'd stopped typing, offered me a mild, friendly smile. With lifted eyebrows and sympathetic eyes. "No, I'm sorry, he isn't. He's out visiting the hospitals and nursing homes today. I can take a message, though."

"Actually, I've left a number of those."

She looked worried now. Suspicious? "You're the lady that calls. Susan."

My shoulders went rigid. Why would she seem suspicious? Had I been too desperate? Too crazy? Was that how I'd come to earn the title there, The Lady that Calls? "I'm Susan, yes, and I've been having something of a faith struggle."

Or—and this was a new thought for me—did my illness that day mar my impression of her?

"That's difficult, I'm sure," she said. "Unfortunately, the pastor can't meet with you today. But I can tell him you came by and are needing to see him."

When I looked at her even expression—pleasant still, but wary now—at her short, curly hair and at the shine of her glasses, when I saw this tidy woman behind her tidy desk, I was thinking of God. "What if I joined your church? Would that make a difference?"

Her eyes flared. Cooled. "We minister to everybody whether they're members here or not. But no, that doesn't make any difference regarding the pastor's schedule."

I could not shake the feeling I was being avoided. "Does he ever check his messages?" I didn't think that I dreamed up her discomfort.

Her mouth had narrowed to the tiniest of points. "Ma'am, I give him the messages. I give him all the messages."

The walls in that room were cream, and the carpet was gold.

The air smelled like plastic flowers.

"All I can say," the secretary said, "is that I'm sorry, but there's nothing I can do."

Those walls and that floor. I would always remember.

"I see. Thank you."

I turned on my heel before she could say anything else.

I'd lost my mind. I could lose my whole career. I was losing my husband, my son. And God did not seem to care.

I was out of that room and down the wavering hall. My shoes knocked against the hard floor, echoing.

I wasn't called to do anything, write anything, be anything.

My body jerked its way out of the building. My feet clanged across the parking lot.

You showed me what I could be. Did you trick me, on purpose? Did you lie?

I wrenched open the car door and hurtled myself into the seat.

I slammed the door with a mighty boom.

I *am finished speaking to you.*

////// //// ////// // ////////

Excerpted from the writings of Anna Maria Magdalena
Muller, November 6, 1807
Copied into my notebook, May, 2005

. . . *[D]*oes anyone care to know what this life has visited upon my dear brother and family? Not alone the fearful acts committed by those who would trespass at midnight and stay nameless to us, but as well the hardness and bitterness with which some, who choose to keep their faces shown, would greet them?

Who cares to know of the deep suffering of silence and long nights, which can neither be seen nor experienced, in truth, save by those who are very near?

I believe all scorn and calumny ought truly be laid at my own door.

This solitary life has not been my own, but God's to give, and on my bed I give thanks to God always for what He has given, for so we are commanded. Still I search my heart to its very bottom for the words I give to God, for ofttimes they come with great anguish and with hot salt tears where I lie.

How hard it is neither to be believed nor regarded by those we wish to think well of us! How hard it is to explain what cannot be explained, how holy Christ could come and speak to this ordinary vessel such things as He has done.

And so I go without adornment and vanity of a woman's hair and without husband in obedience to God. And none do ask, neither holy Christ nor any of my fellow men, if it is my special wish so to live. It is my lot and my cross, and I give God thanks as is due Him.

Yet ofttimes I consider this cross to be ponderous and grievous to carry, and consider it fortunate none do ask, for truly, in my heart's deeps of great darkness, I know not the words I would submit in return. . . .

////// //// ////// // ////////

When I drove my car up the long gravel drive—the late morning blinding on the land—and I witnessed that little, white house slowly expanding, I felt cold and hollow inside, as though in me coiled blank, endless corridors saturated with an air-conditioned moan.

I'd come to unlock the house. No casual check like those over the years to make sure the heat worked, pipes were unfrozen, trees hadn't fallen, the house was still there.

The movers were on their way. I'd come to stay.

Soon after the movers arrived, Samuel did too, with subs and chips and Ian.

Dining options were limited in Clemtown, and Samuel had offered to bring food for the movers and me. I'd thanked him as icily as I could and requested he please bring Ian, so Ian could get used to the idea of Mommy's house.

"You've said what you're going to do," I'd told Samuel. "But I have a right to see my son."

The chancellor's face had shifted to a meticulous emptiness. I'd get nothing more from his face, ever again.

I took a splintering, shivering shock every time I saw and comprehended this.

Vestiges of dislike had been in his eyes, but he'd consented.

The movers seemed pleased at the sight of the food bags Samuel brought. The tired men who'd come at sunup to the other house to extract my belongings sagged and slumped themselves onto the porch. They unwrapped their sandwiches and ate.

I went with Samuel and Ian into the house. It smelled of old. It smelled of stale and of sticky heat.

Ian galloped in, his shoes thunking against the wood floor, Lammykin lolling under his arm. He lobbed a wordless shout into the air, ricocheting his voice as far as it would go. "That big," he said, as though surprised.

Samuel set the final bag of lunch on the end table in the living room.

"Come here, baby," I said to Ian.

He went clopping into the back hall. "Hello?" reverberated along the walls.

"Ian," said Samuel. "Come back here, please."

Ian peeped around the doorframe.

"We're going to eat," I said. "Then we'll see Mommy's house."

Thrumming, curious, Ian paused there. "Mommy's house?"

Samuel relocated his attention to me. "We're not eating here."

"What?" came out of me before I could stop it. An absurdity to ask.

So the bag on the table had one sandwich only. For me.

"Don't do this," said Samuel.

"What?" I said. "What am I doing?"

"No, no," said Ian, his feet drumming into the room, slinging his finger toward me. "No, no, stop it."

I squatted. So I could speak to him on the level. So I could continue to function in that room without shrieking obscenities at my child's father.

"Give me a hug, please, Ian. You and Daddy are going to go eat together."

Samuel said, "How would you like to go to McDonald's?"

The pit of my stomach crinkled and turned cold. I abhorred McDonald's.

Samuel was bribing Ian to return to Millsborough with McDonald's.

I was staying here.

"Go McDonald's?" Ian looked doubtful.

I put my knees to the floor to steady myself. I brightened my voice. "You and Daddy can go and eat McDonald's. Mommy's going to eat here while the men move Mommy's things into Mommy's house."

"Okay." Ian gave a vigorous nod. "I eat McDonald's and Daddy. Lammykin, too."

"Yes," I said. "Give me a big hug, baby, before you and Lammykin go with Daddy."

Ian pitched, launched himself into me. I sat hard and clutched him and thought I would shudder into pieces from the sobs I did not make.

"As soon as Mommy gets her house ready," I said, "you can come back and sleep here." I didn't dare look at Samuel.

Ian said, "I want sleep Mommy's house."

"All right, let's go, son," Samuel said. "Daddy's hungry, and I'd say Ian's probably hungry, too."

"Yep, I hungry, too," Ian was saying as I kissed his soft, smooth forehead and turned him loose.

"Bye, Ian," I said. "See you after a while."

Samuel was already at the door. Ian clomped away with Lammykin flopping, and the door opened onto the sound of the men talking, and then they were gone.

I sat unmoving except for the hard, shaking grieving that wracked me. I hissed and sibilated as quietly as I could until I heard Samuel's car start and then crunch away down the drive.

I jumped up, crying harder now, and grabbed the sandwich shop bag. I ran through the house to the bathroom, where I jerked the wrapping from my sandwich—a six-inch turkey on dark bread with provolone, tomato, lettuce, and onion, cucumber slices and brown pub mustard—the sandwich my husband had ordered for me, and I dumped it into the commode and flushed the toilet.

The toilet was clogged now. I was stupid and furious and hungry.

I would believe God had damned this day. If I still believed in God.

////// //// ////// // ////////

When I awoke, sunrise was not yet in the room. A low, gray glow intimated that something was on the way.

As soon as my eyes had opened, sleep left me as if it had never come. I tossed back the sheet and traipsed to the front door in my sweatpants.

I wasn't a late riser usually. Neither was I someone who watched the sun appear. Now I had no idea what person I was.

I opened the door onto a hushed and purple world. Entered.

The September air thrummed with insect rattles. A rooster crowed in the distance. The mountains were smudges of dark. The sky was tinged at the eastern rim with scant streaks of scarlet and gold.

I sat on the edge of the porch. I watched red overtake the sky.

This was what life would be like without my mind.

No husband. No child. No God.

The wind began to move, stirring the hair near my face.

The pain of being without them went so very deep.

I watched the long front yard revealed as it stretched out to the road. Everything reabsorbed its everyday colors. I saw the dark rows of evergreens that lined the long gravel drive. I saw the smooth patch of ground, grassy now, where Mamaw had kept her garden.

I saw the view I'd seen as a child, recognizable still, but turned strange.

It was like being consigned to hell. I never dreamed I'd come back to this place.

Was my presence here Samuel's doing? God's? Had I done this to myself?

Because I did not have to be in Clemtown. I could've made demands, I supposed.

If there was anything I could want except that this illness, this divorce, would not be happening.

A dog barked somewhere off across the field, to the west. Birdsong livened the sky.

And yet to me there was a sort of sacred contrariness in being here.

(Sacred, as in, a time set apart. Contrary, as in, fuck you, I'm sick.)

If I believed sacredness existed anymore.

Motion coming from the west across the field focused my attention on a small creature gamboling toward the house. A little goat trotted into the yard, a little clumsily, and paused in front of the porch. It looked at me and bleated, an eerie, humanlike sound.

"You're in the wrong place," I said.

The little goat looked at me out of its weird eyes. The barking grew louder.

"I think somebody's looking for you." I slid off the porch and into the wet grass.

The goat jumped away from me, bleating, stumbling. Its left front leg unsteady.

"Come here," I said in the voice I used with Ian. I had no idea how to corner a goat. Even if this one might be hurt.

The goat tottered. Appeared good-natured, with bright eyes and an expression like a smile. But it did not come to me.

This encounter upended expectations of mine for certain. I'd always associated this community with cows.

The barking dog got nearer still. A man's voice seemed to be calling, "Maggie?" I didn't know which had the name, the goat or the dog.

"Are you Maggie?" I said.

The goat just smiled at me.

The dog came galloping, then, and the goat tried to flee, but the dog swept around to hem it and herd it. The goat dodged back westward, and the dog chased it toward the man's voice.

I peered where the animals were headed. The man waved. He kept walking nearer, though his goat and his dog continued home.

"Hello, there!" he shouted.

I stayed with folded arms, conscious of my lack of proper clothes. When he was near enough for us to talk in ordinary speaking voices, I said, "Is Maggie the goat?"

"Yes, she's a problem child. Sorry about that." The man seemed both genial and energetic, the sort who probably awakened early every day of his life. "I'm Luther Stafford. My wife and I decided we'd try raising goats a little over a year ago. We'd probably do it again if we had to do it over, but there's been quite a learning curve."

"I can imagine," I said, though I couldn't. "I'm Susan Huffman. I grew up here." Luther's name was a thing I should know. I searched my brain to match his mannerisms with memories.

"You know, we may have met," he said. "I used to visit my grandparents in the summers. Down by the store?"

"Oh, yes, hello." I nodded, recalling an older couple that Ben and Hulda Huffman had hailed and spoken to often. "Maggie looked like she might have hurt herself making her escape. I hope she'll be all right."

Maggie was odd and sprightly and spunky. I decided I liked her.

"Thanks, don't worry, I'll check her out." Luther gestured at the expanse of field he'd crossed. "Mona's over there putting a casserole together to bring you later on. But if you want to come on over for breakfast, you can get your casserole yourself."

I was surprised by the invitation. I'd always thought of breakfast as a meal for family. "Why, yes, thank you. Let me go run a comb through my hair first."

As soon as I said that, I wondered why I had. Mamaw had used that expression when she'd meant to make herself more presentable. I was not used to hearing it come out of my own mouth.

"Sure. I'll let Mona know to expect you."

Dazed by the series of strange, rapid happenings, I returned to the inside of my house.

"Welcome," said Mona when I entered her lemon-hued kitchen. She had an accent, from up North somewhere, or maybe it was Midwestern.

"Thank you for having me," I said. Luther sat at the table, which was set with breakfast. The room smelled rich with bacon and oranges and with baking.

"Your casserole is in the oven," said Mona, by the sink. "Chicken and potatoes. It should make a few meals for you."

I wondered when Luther and Mona had settled in Clemtown, how they'd come to this house where the older Staffords had never lived.

"It smells wonderful," I said. "Thank you." I did not want to be in this kitchen. I wanted my own kitchen, my old kitchen.

Washing her hands, Mona looked at me over her shoulder. "We're glad to have you as our new neighbor." Her smile was reassuring and friendly but did not overwhelm me with closeness.

I attempted to smile in return. The past days had so unmoored me I could hardly see how I belonged to anyone, belonged anywhere, even in a role as simple as neighbor.

Luther gestured to a chair and a place setting where a mug steamed with coffee. "Maggie did cut her leg jumping out of that pen," he said to me. "She ought to be fine, though, if she'll behave."

"That's good to hear." I sat at the table as well, considering the costs of behavior, to goats and to women both. I wanted Maggie safe, of course, but I'd liked her free.

Then Mona joined us, sliding effortlessly into the chair at my right hand, and began to say grace over the food and over us. My neck and shoulders stiff, my insides hard, I braced myself against her words, for I was not about to join in any prayer to any God that had put me here. But I tried to restrain myself with respect. At a table of eggs and bacon, bagels and cream cheese, Yankees and native East Tennesseans, I tried to feel myself as present in a place that was trying to welcome me against my wishes, as an outsider who was being warmly drawn into a circle I had fervently believed would block me out.

////// //// ////// // ////////

*T*hat evening, I was carrying a warmed slice of casserole into the living room to eat and watch the news. Before I could sit on the couch, however, out the window I spied a woman in a skirt and blouse walking up the driveway with some Saran-wrap-covered package.

I was about to be the recipient of a neighborly advance.

I put down the plate and went to the door to meet her.

She had on pantyhose, I could see, in that heat—paired with flats, at least, and not heels—and was bringing me a plate of food. Treats of some kind.

In the way she moved, the shape of her smile, she looked vaguely familiar.

"Hi, there, I'm Joy Pridemore," she said. "You're Susan Huffman, right? I don't know if you remember me from school? I was Joy Boggs then. My mamaw lived by you all."

"Oh, yes," I said, remembering the name more than the classmate.

"Welcome! We're so glad to have you here in Clemtown. I brought you all some lemon bars."

She handed over the Saran-wrapped paper plate as if it was heaped with gold, and the desserts did look delicious, sifted with powdered sugar. What I needed to add to my extra weight.

"How very thoughtful of you," I said. "Thank you."

Joy could now commence to being my neighbor and did exactly that. "Was that your husband and little boy yesterday when you all were moving?"

"Yes. You won't be seeing as much of them," I said. "It's going to be me for a while."

I witnessed, like exclamations in her eyes, her sudden, sharp consciousness, a moment of faltering.

"Well," she said, "you know the Collinses don't live on the other side of you anymore, they sold their place to Wally Stafford's youngest grandson and his wife. They're a little peculiar, she's from up North, you know. But good people anyhow."

"That's good to know." Gladly I switched along with Joy's deliberate change of subject. Certain that I too was going to end up *a little peculiar* in this community. If I was lucky.

"Now, if you're looking for a church," said Joy, "our church is having a picnic in about a month, after worship. Like an old-time dinner on the grounds. Give you time to get situated and all first. You'd sure be welcome."

A church was the very last thing I was looking for. "I appreciate the invitation, Joy. And the lemon bars, very much. They look wonderful."

"Oh, I was sure glad to do it! Let us know if there's any way we can help you get settled in."

Joy exited the porch sedately, leaving me with unnecessary dessert, an unsought invitation, and a backhanded compliment of my other neighbors.

I carried the paper plate indoors.

Her casual-visit outfit had scorched and smothered me just to see it.

I placed the plate of dessert on the kitchen table and admired the beautiful food.

I could not fathom the look of the world through Joy's eyes. But there was a person there.

No less than the Lindseys of the world, I realized. No less than me.

Because, I was beginning to believe, if God existed, we'd all been abandoned alike.

(I chose a bar from beneath the plastic wrap, snaked it out. I bit into the burst of lemon, the heady sweetness.)

In Lindsey's case, in Joy's case, I simply did not know how.

///// //// ///// // ////////

The next day, Sunday, in Millsborough, I took out of the bank account I shared with my husband the least amount of money I could to buy groceries.

I had no income now. Only a checkbook and an ATM card. I was angry enough, vengeful enough, to fantasize cleaning out the account's contents. But in my real, true life, I dreaded scrutiny of any expenses not strictly for basic living. I was terrified to do the wrong thing. Take what wasn't mine, what was not yet decreed as mine. Jeopardize my standing with the law, perhaps.

Forfeit any hope of seeing my son.

I bought my groceries in Millsborough, too, in a place far from Samuel's house, not yet ready to shop in Clemtown's tiny store and become the focus of everyone's wonder.

Back at Mamaw's and Papaw's, I stowed my food and necessaries in the cabinets. In the ancient refrigerator that had been lugged out of storage.

I did not know how long that refrigerator could go on working.

I lived in a house and drove a car with no certainty I would eventually own either one.

The precariousness of my life became blindingly real three days later, when I went to the mailbox and discovered inside it an official piece of mail commanding I was

Not to see Ian

At all.

I had no breath or blood
Hands or warmth
Tears or voice.
I was insubstantial and nowhere.

If I wanted a different outcome, the injunction informed me, I would have to appear in fifteen days and plead my case.

I could not find my way out of my head.
I'd thought there'd be more time than this.
I'd understood a special judge, a retired judge, would be appointed to handle our divorce.
So I had no lawyer yet. And didn't know if I had the means to secure one.

////// //// ////// // ////////

Nell called me back that same afternoon.
"Listen," she said, "I'm coming to see you. And Old Sarah wants to come with me. Will that be all right with you?"
I'd been sitting on the couch staring at nothing.
"Please," I said. "Yes."
When I hadn't been pacing the house, shrieking at Samuel, yelling at no one.
When Nell and Old Sarah got there, I met them at the door.

The floor plummeted away endlessly beneath my feet.

Nell hugged me. Old Sarah hugged me.

"Don't you let him make you think you haven't been good with Ian," said Old Sarah. "You've always been good with Ian."

I began to cry, uttering sounds I had never made before in my life.

Then I was sitting on the couch, and Nell was beside me.

"Susan, we'll testify," she said. "Jim and I. If that will benefit you."

I pressed my fists against the cushion. Nell was the friend I'd confessed my crimes to. I cringed at what she might be asked to reveal.

"And I'll tell them what I've seen," said Old Sarah from the lumpy armchair. "What a good mother you are."

My head was lowered. "Thank you." I'd been an execrable mother.

"I know some organizations that may help," said Nell. "We can get you legal advice."

I sagged further. "I don't want *organizations*, Nell. Samuel hears divorce cases every day—what doesn't he know about all this? I want a real lawyer. I have to have a real lawyer who will fight a real fight, or there is no telling when I will get to see Ian while the rest of this divorce mess all drags on."

The smell of the morning's coffee and omelet still lingered. I hadn't been hungry since.

"Take the money and get you one," said Old Sarah.

"I'm scared to do that," I admitted. "How much is too much?"

Nell patted my shoulder. I wiped the back of my hand across my face.

"Nell has news," said Old Sarah. "I think you should know it."

I gazed fearfully at my friend, who was doing the same with me.

"Lorraine's separated from her husband," she said.

"What?" I was genuinely shocked.

And then I wasn't.

"She's playing in a band now," said Old Sarah. "*Lady and the Giantkillers*, I believe."

"Well," I said. "Good for her."

I did not doubt that Lorraine would not be appearing on my doorstep. Wishing to console me. Offering her testimony.

She'd been at the party. She'd witnessed the spectacular argument and could attest to my derangement. She'd been at the center of it, in fact.

She'd been working her way to the center of everything, all along.

I didn't need God to show me that.

///// //// ///// // ///////

*I*f I'd encountered bad days before, days when I could barely force my way out of the bed and onto my feet, days when I could hardly dress myself or brush my hair—the *honey-colored cloud* of my hair, as Samuel used to speak of it to others, as he used to see it—then I could only laugh now at how bitterly hard I had believed such days to be.

If I'd been able to laugh, that is.

I had no reason to get up. I had nowhere to turn.

Yet somewhere—deep in the bedrock of myself, perhaps—I found a small nudge.

It was almost imperceptible.

Thoroughly inexplicable.

But it was there.

Each day I tried to do something, some small thing.

I brushed my teeth.

Or I climbed in the tub and bathed.

I made myself put bread in the toaster.

I made myself eat the toast.

Even if that was all I could do that day.

On the very worst day I endured, I dragged the curtains open. I sprawled among the sheets and let the sunlight wash over me.

I had to survive this.

I had to show Samuel how wrong he was. I was going to stabilize, return to my work, learn to live with my disease.

I had to convince a judge I was well enough to care for my son.

If God had been there with me, I would have searched my Bible for comfort.

Prayed for guidance and strength.

How I wished God was there.

But the only presence I could feel was the bristling, mile-high barricade of my anger. My wounding. My betrayal.

My illness.

///// //// ///// // ///////

I imagine that Ian and I are at the Staffords'.

I take him out back to see the goats.

Ian's giddy to see the animals darting about in the pen and coming toward the fence and bleating as though begging to be seen. He glances up at me. He laughs and runs to them.

"Look at all the goats, Ian," I say.

"I pet them, Mommy," he says.

Maggie is the one who comes closest. Because I'm concerned the goats might butt at him through the fence, I lift him and take him through the gate, so he can pat Maggie's back.

Naturally, in my imaginings, she comes right to us.

"Be soft," I say to Ian.

He puts out his hand and musses with her hair. Maggie does not complain, just looks at him with those weird, rectangular-pupil eyes.

"She nice," he says. "Good, good goat."

I'm grateful to Maggie for this moment. I squeeze him tight and imagine we can do this forever.

///// //// ///// // ///////

"*I*'m awful," I said to Annika, "that's how I am. Afraid I'm never going to see my son again. That he's going to grow up without me and will never remember me." I had to dig violently in my pocketbook for Kleenex. "I thought I knew my husband. Now the only thing I can do is despise him."

"That's entirely understandable, that you might feel that way," said Annika. "Can you do anything constructive to affect what's happening to you? Are there productive steps you could take to help you cope better?"

"I can cry," I said.

I applied the Kleenex.

"My friend told me," I went on, "about a place that gives legal advice for—people with limited ability to pay. I guess I could call them."

I tried to wrangle the dark miasma of my thoughts into shapes of words.

"I could call attorneys' offices," I said, "maybe some good soul would take my case, since maybe, surely, I'll have a little money to call my own one of these days. I don't think Samuel means to fight me about that in the end, I don't, but neither do I want to open myself to any accusations right now, about money or anything else. And I don't want to rush things, but maybe I can manage to go back to work before long. If they'll take me back."

"Of course you don't want to rush things," said Annika. "You want to go back when you're ready."

I wanted to be ready. "It's just that it's really hard to bear up under it all. All that's been happening to me." I did not believe I had ever confessed so much fear, so much grief, to another human being in my life.

"What else?" she said. "What are you doing to help you get through this?"

I looked at the rainbow-colored pictures on her walls. Tried to breathe in the calm and the sanctity of her space, which had its own scent, a scent of rugs and books and furniture polish.

"I'm letting myself get as much sleep as I need, that's probably a bad thing." Staying in bed for twelve hours together was generally not recommended for people with bipolar. "When I can clean around the house, that helps, it feels good actually, since I'm not thinking as much when I do that."

Annika, who'd been writing surreptitiously during our conversation, nodded.

A welcome sight.

"I do try to make myself do something each day," I added.

I was glad to see anybody say yes to me, hear me out, encourage me to stay tethered to this planet and not go hurtling through space all alone.

"That's a start," she said.

///// //// ///// // ///////

I was at home in my terry bathrobe, the color of butterscotch, reading, when I first learned some people with bipolar can experience *psychosis* as part of their illness—a fact of which I'd been entirely unaware.

I had driven to Millsborough after seeing Annika—thinking to improve my situation in some small way—and had checked out books using my library card.

Where I no longer lived.

And where my card was no longer valid.

I felt like an outlaw. I had never perpetrated such a fraud in my life.

I did not care.

Until the moment in my bathrobe, reading, I'd always assumed psychosis was a schizophrenic thing.

A state of mind I would never share.

The page was soaked in sunlight, I remember

My bare feet on the floor

I discovered that psychosis in bipolar people could manifest as

Religious delusion

For instance

I clutched the book

Shocked

Aghast

Aware

Like someone had rushed at my knees, knocked me sideways and down.

The blow resonated through me. The bruising covered every muscle and bone.

It did not matter that I was not speaking to God, that I already doubted what I'd passionately believed.

I had to revise my understanding of everything that had taken place since February.

The cross. The table. The commission. The worship services.

What I'd seen with my eyes, heard with my ears.

Felt in my core.

My experiences. The real lived life of me.

All the insights
The beautiful feelings
The creeping suspicions
None had been anything. Meant anything.

I kept on sitting there, holding the book.

My heart was spurting and dumping all the blood in my body onto the floor.

There was no *special.* No deep love coming to me or to anyone from the far reaches of the universe.

Mamaw was mistaken. Anna Maria Magdalena had to have been a crazy woman, I understood now.

Like me.

I picked up my Bible. I picked up the notebook I'd believed contained revelations from God about my life.

I was mortified and disgusted to look at them now.

I could rip them into pieces so small they could never be reconstructed. I could set them on fire or hurl them into the pond from the shade of the cedars to make them sink from sight.

But I have deep, deep aversion to destroying books. Of any kind.

So I went into the bedroom that had been my father's when he was a boy.

My mother's, when she and I lived here.

I did not intend to spend much time in this room.

I opened the cedar-lined closet and tugged the overhead chain to turn on the light.

In the back corner slouched a giant, floppy doll with a grotesque plastic head, grinning. It belonged to an aunt I had no memory of.

I reached up and shoved the books as far as I could. To the back of the shelf, the back of the closet. I heard the rasp. The thump.

I pulled the chain again, and the light clicked off.

The shadow of the doll solidified.

Loomed.

I shut the door and walked away.

///// //// ////// // ////////

"**W**ell, looky there!" A great, mirthless grin burgeoned onto the face of the portly woman behind the counter. "If it isn't old Sue!"

I stopped inside the door.

Though she'd neglected to say the rest of the nickname, I had no trouble grasping the allusion.

There were variations, of course. *Stuck-up Sue. Smartypants Sue.*

"Hello, Roberta." I approached the counter. I needed to pay for my gas.

"This beats all!" Roberta's eyes quivered with gleams of savage delight. "What're you doing here in Clemtown?"

Her face resumed the insolent look I remembered from childhood. She wore the same shade of eyeshadow.

I was fourteen again.

"I'm at Mamaw's and Papaw's for a while." I handed her the five.

I was awestruck how an encounter between two people could annihilate time, could nullify every aspect of our lives except this one, the one in which each of us had been powerless to change our circumstances as children, the one in which she had inflicted the brickbat of her pain and insecurity on me.

She took the money. She stood there holding it. "For a while? You mean, to stay?"

The air in the place smelled close and rank, like old grease and cloying pink air freshener. "For a while, yes."

She hooted, put the bill in the register. "Guess you're the same as the rest of us now."

She closed the drawer. The eyes on me again, leering.

I'd never imagined such a judgment rendered on my life.

That I was deemed to be such a bitch as to believe I was more worthy than my childhood peers

That this belief actually existed in me and I was condemned now to the twin horrors of realizing this and witnessing that certitude destroyed.

I would later learn her husband was out of work and on drugs and her father was in prison.

Her smile for me was ruthless nevertheless.

"Welcome back," she said.

///// //// ///// // ///////

To distract myself from my trouble, to focus myself, I was laying shelf paper in 1950s metal kitchen cabinets in my unairconditioned house.

I'd opened the windows, and two large box fans spun hot air from one side of the house to the other. There were no ceiling fans. I was in an old T-shirt and denim shorts, and I'd worked up a considerable sweat measuring and scissoring. It had been a manic sort of day, and I'd decided after this project I was going to soak in a bubble bath and try to level off, to the degree that I could, when I heard a car scrabbling up the gravel drive.

I wasn't expecting anyone. I kept working.

A tap-and-rattle soon quivered the screen door at the front, which I heard rather than saw.

So I went to the front door to see.

The old wooden door was closed and locked. I was not yet used to living alone in the country. The door had no peephole, so I shifted the curtains and sheers and peeked out the living room window.

Hugh Mackey was on the porch.

I snatched myself away.

I felt like I'd just spied a zebra grazing alongside cows across the lane.

I struggled to explain what he was doing there.

In the time I'd had before the move, I'd tried to right things as well as I could. I'd sent him all I'd done for the symposium, ashamed to discover how little there was. In the e-mail, I'd explained I was going to be away.

But I hadn't disclosed where that would be.

The tap-and-rattle vibrated the door once more. Startled me.

He had every right to yell in my face if he wanted. I answered the door.

"Dr. Mackey," I said.

"Susan? I got your e-mail." He registered my presence gingerly, as though he was not quite clear who he'd found.

"Yes, Hugh—" I wanted not to wince, but did. "—I'm sorry. I hope I didn't sabotage the symposium past saving."

"Don't worry about that. Are you all right?"

"How did you find me?"

"I'm a researcher. I made inquiries. Are you all right?"

Wherever we were headed, I wasn't sure I wanted to go. I folded my arms. "I'm alive."

"They said you were sick."

"Yes."

We looked at each other a long moment. He shook his head. "I should have realized you were in trouble. I should have done something."

"Hugh, that's very kind." I felt us veering a dangerous way. "But there would be no reason for you to realize or to do anything."

"Just tell me this." He spread his hands. "Is he actually leaving you when you're so sick you can't even work?"

I wanted to say it was none of his business. I knew then that I would field variations on this question for the rest of my life. "Where did you hear that?"

"There's no way not to hear it."

A sudden rush of scalding prickling like bee stings over-powered my sight.

"I knew it," said Hugh. "He's a son of a bitch."

I blinked to clear my vision. "Stop, damn it, you don't know anything about this." He had no knowledge of my pain, my husband. My hand touched my eyes.

"Yes, I do. I know you."

We faced each other as I let what he'd said soak into my brain, my sweat-slick body.

My arms were limp at my sides.

In the arrhythmic pulse of an instant, my hands had seized his collar.

It happened without my volition.

Except volition was all I was.

And he was not stopping me.

I kissed him. He did not stop that, either.

We were kissing and coming into the house.

The door was shoved shut.

I could not keep track of what was happening. I was almost not there.

He had hold of me, saying my name. I fumbled with his buttons. He'd taken off his glasses. Frantic hands grabbed and clutched everywhere. I was a loud surge of confusion and of wanting.

Until my shirt came off over my head, and then I was a bolt of panic.

"Jesus, oh, Christ, Hugh." I yanked away and sat on the couch, my hands to my temples, looking at the wood beneath my feet.

"What is it?" he said in the most forlorn voice. "You don't have to love me. I don't care."

I did not want the enormity of his feelings or the risk of damaging them.

And now I feared who might have seen me drag Hugh into the house. Feared who might be called upon to attest to how unbalanced I'd become.

My fingers spread into my hair. "Don't you see—he's going to use anything—anything at all, anything he can—to keep me from seeing my son."

I tried to reason with myself. I tried to persuade myself no one in Clemtown would bother to tell Samuel my goings and comings.

"That's terrible," said Hugh. "Unbelievable."

"I have to be—so careful." I had no idea what I wanted. Except Ian. "I'm sorry, I'm so sorry."

The house hummed with box fans, but heat trickled down my back, slicked my forehead.

"I understand," he said. And then, "I shouldn't have come. I see that now, that this was a bad time. I only wanted to know that you were all right."

"As you can see, I'm not."

"You're going to be all right if you want to be. I know what a fighter you are."

What Hugh said irked me, a hot slice to my chest. I wasn't ill for lack of wanting to be well. But I knew he'd meant his words to be kind.

I looked up. It was a difficult sight. "Thank you for coming, Hugh." I didn't know if I would see the sight again, his face, this colleague of mine.

He shifted his shoulders like a shrug, like he meant to sidle and slide out of the house. He was putting his buttons right. "I hope you get well soon."

The door was closing, then, closing him out, and I was on the other side, in my shorts and my bra, in solitude, in Clemtown.

////// //// ////// // ////////

*I*n a procession of hot, muggy, gray, and rainy days, this was one more.

Closer to the court date.

The sky seemed low and heavy enough to crush the earth.

The trees seemed to be squeezing water from their branches to spray and spew all over the world.

I got myself in the car and drove to Millsborough.

Windshield wipers clicked and whipped.

I drove to the liquor store and bought a bottle of wine.

I bought a corkscrew, too, because who knew where mine was or if I even had one in a box or a drawer anyplace in the house.

Because of my medication, I was not supposed to drink anymore.

However I did not give a fuck.

I drove home.

Actually, no, it was not *home*, I drove back to Clemtown.

I was pretty sure I had no wine glass, but that, at least, was one problem I could solve.

I drank straight from the bottle.

The room tilted and rolled.

I wanted every detail of it to melt from my mind.

Somewhere along the way I recognized I might be risking my life, mixing medication and alcohol inside of me.

And wondered what would become of Ian after I died.

I was extremely drunk and panicked now.

I lay down on the floor. In that sweltering room, the rain crashing down outside, I could hear the wood sighing. I could hear the house groaning.

I took off all my clothes.

I had no stamina to go running through the yard in the rain.

I had no ability to scream or rage.

I sang *In the Pines*. I sang the saddest songs I could remember.

Finally I had to go throw up. I pitched and reeled into the bathroom.

This would be how it would end for me.

Wasted.

Out of my mind.

I vomited my guts into the toilet.

God in heaven, I thought.

I sank to my knees, collapsed on the floor.

Fat and naked and pathetic and ridiculous.

God in heaven.

God in heaven.

///// //// ////// // ////////

My mailbox had turned into a source of trepidation for me now.

So when I opened it and saw the envelope addressed to me, with no return address, I was wary. I was agitated.

I didn't know what it could mean.

When I reached the porch and opened the envelope

When I glimpsed the cashier's check inside for four thousand dollars

I had to sit down.

I looked at the check without seeing it until I could see it again.

Air moved in and out of my lungs. The day smelled of dusty grass.

I wondered even harder what this piece of mail meant.

I tried to conceive of who had sent this to me.

Jim and Nell. Nate and Charles. All my old circle of friends.

Dr. Rickwell. My colleagues at the college.

It could be any of them, all of them, none of them.

But I knew who it was not. It was not God.

Could not be God, the God who did not exist.

It was human beings doing what God ought to have done.

Doing what I was desirous, ashamed to have them do.

The envelope crinkled in my hands.
It was difficult not to feel shame.
I tried.
I drew out the crisp, stiff check.

This was the look of mercy.

I could now retain a real lawyer until the judge decided what funds I'd be allowed to access, pending the outcome of the divorce.
I could fight to show I was not a danger to my son.

////// //// ////// // ////////

When I think of my first day in court, here is what comes to mind:
The stern, dark-paneled walls, which sapped all light from the room, the same way the earth can drink water endlessly that falls from the sky.
The dank, sad smell in there.
The pinch of my shoes.
The gaping, turbulent emptiness that seeped from behind my ribs and pooled at my middle.
The unfamiliar face of the judge.
The barely familiar face of my attorney.

The sharp, serious face of Samuel's attorney, whom I did not know.

(I would later learn this man had worked with Samuel in a firm years ago, when the two were just starting out, and now this man lived and practiced high-powered, tough-fisted law in Nashville.)

The earnest faces of Nell and Annika, Charles and Old Sarah, as they told the mostly vacant courtroom what they knew about me. How I was fervently working toward stability and was a menace to no one. Least of all the little boy I loved. Whatever stray glimmers of light that did not sink into the walls, lingered on their faces, until they paled and shone like ghosts.

Samuel's constant refusal to meet my eyes at any moment during the proceedings. Instead of looking into my face, he would look at my shoulder or at someplace beside my head.

My own husband, Chancellor Ellison, testifying against me, recalling the night he'd come home from work to find me struggling with Ian in the upstairs bathroom.

The rumblings of my own mind, telling me I was not wanted here, that I would never again be in command of my own faculties, that the judge would never find me more convincing than my eminent husband, that I was bound to fail.

But what I remember most of all—the part I replayed until I'd worn it to tatters in my head—was the sight of Lorraine, in her linen-colored suit, her brown eyes eager and sincere, as she spoke to Samuel's attorney on Samuel's behalf:

"Yes, sir, that evening at the party, it did frighten me, and it concerned me very much—not for myself, you understand, but for Dr. Huffman—to have her accuse me in that way, without any evidence at all."

She turned from the attorney to the judge and back again as she spoke.

What I could scarcely take in, what floated up in my mind as I watched her, was that this was no performance, it could not be anything but her barest honesty, not with the transparent look in her eyes, and with her every word so scrupulous and clean, even as I sat there and hated everything she was and ever could be, even as she turned and looked straight into my face with those guileless eyes and said:

"Because I never intended to hurt her. I was her friend. I was her friend from the very first."

////// //// ////// // ///////

*I*n the end, however, I did not fail.

The judge decided I was not about to harm Ian and I'd be allowed to have my son at my home in accordance with the local rules.

Which meant, in general, seeing him every other weekend, and from Tuesday night through Wednesday evening on the alternating week.

Thanksgiving, Christmas, Father's Day, Mother's Day, were exceptions spelled out in ponderous detail in the rules.

All this, provided I adhered to my psychiatrist appointments and my therapist appointments and my treatment regimen to the satisfaction of the court.

This, until our divorce was finalized.

So, of course, this wasn't really the end.

It was actually, most probably, only the beginning.

///// //// ///// // ////////

At a secondhand store in Millsborough, I find a blanket covered in circus animals. Not too faded, not ugly. It's reasonably cheerful.

I find a wooden toy chest that has seen better days.

Nell brings me a set of bed rails and will not tell me how much she paid.

I take down the outdoorsy prints from the walls of my childhood bedroom and store them in the attic.

Nate and Charles come and help me paint, hang shelves. They say they have a friend who's an interior decorator, and they obtained the supplies from her at special friend prices.

I'm not sure which parts of their story are true.

We put up a picture in primary colors, from the thrift shop in Clemtown. A boy and his dog.

It is hard to feel as threadbare as I do, looking at the rehabilitated room.

Somewhere on the far side of this feeling, I thank my friends.

Soon I'll find out what money I'll be allowed to live on until the divorce is done. Then I'll buy a DVD player, toys for the empty chest, reimburse my friends what I've tallied as best I can.

In the meantime, here I am.

I'm ready to receive my son.

///// //// ///// // ///////

When I arrive to get Ian one weekend, he springs from his play and embraces my leg. I crouch and hug him back.

"It's good to see you, baby," I say. "Are you ready to come with Mommy?"

"No, play," he says, pulling away.

"He's packed up," says Samuel from across the room. "Unless there's some last toy he decides he wants."

"Ian, you want to bring something else?" I say. "Be sure and get Giant and Lammykin." This, though I loathed Lammykin.

"No!" says Ian, sitting firmly down in the midst of his blocks and his stuffed menagerie. "I play here."

I have no idea how to tell my son what's going on with his family, because I can't explain it to myself. I am powerless to make what is happening to us stop.

"Mommy's taking you to Mommy's house." I walk closer. "Don't you want to come with Mommy? It's Ian's turn to come."

Ian kicks at his blocks. They crash and scatter. "Mommy not go! Ian not go, never go!"

"Ian," says Samuel. "You need to calm down."

I kneel, struggling to remain calm myself. "It's okay, honey," I say to Ian. "It's a lot to take in, I know." I reach for him.

"No, you stop make me stop!" He swats at me. Smacks my hand.

All the air is expelled from my lungs.

"Ian!" Samuel covers the distance between us shockingly fast.

My hand does not hurt. Inside my chest is the tender place.

Ian crumples and bawls.

"You will *never* hit your mother," Samuel says, standing over us. "*Never*. Do you understand?"

Ian throws back his head, still crying, and screams to the ends of the earth.

"Shhh." I stand, and I gather him up, and he falls against me, slinging his arms around my neck. "Mommy's here, Ian. Mommy loves you."

He continues to cry in great heaves. My shoulder is thoroughly wet. Beyond his head, I watch Samuel watching, his expression a strange admixture of coolness and guilt and reproach, and it is all I can do not to glower back, to shriek with all my rage, demand to know how this sorry situation will better anyone, in the end or at any time, declare as loudly and emphatically as I am able that *this is all your fault.*

Instead I remain civil. For my son's sake.

I pat Ian's back, making circular motions with the hand he just slapped.

////// //// ////// // ////////

My husband never lived in this house with me, but his absence is always there.

Some days it has more substance than the clothes on my body, the television I tap on with a flick of the remote, the curtains I close.

Most days his absence is more present than I am.

I have to travel through the hours of my days while denying this as best I can.

Over and over I find myself returning—each time I shove it off, and each time it crawls back to me—returning to the moment I knew I wanted to be with Samuel.

It was a day I had late classes, on a morning when I cancelled my office hour, drove from Edenton to Blue, and went into his courtroom.

Because there he was in his robe, like he was a stranger—as he should be to me in that place, that profession, a stranger to everyone—his large hands holding important papers, his eyes taking in the individuals before him, as he listened to the problems of the community, his voice measured, reasoned, but firm and pronounced as he said whatever had to be said.

I could not get over his hands on the papers, his hands on the gavel.

There was nothing he did in that place that was capricious or mindless or selfish. I knew what I was seeing was presence. Was assessment. Was intention.

I'd grown up in a household where I'd always had enough, and yet somehow it was never enough. My mother worked odd schedules, and my mamaw and papaw were aloof and stern and loving in the way of many Appalachian grandparents, and I had no good memory of my runaway father, only the few photographs of his boyhood and young adulthood on the walls of his parents' house. With my books and my own dreams of escape, I'd had to sustain myself through the long hours of every day, as most of the adults in my life let me drop through one crack and another.

But in Chancellor Ellison's hands, I would be safe. From where I sat in the back of the courtroom, watching him conduct himself capably in the handling of other people's mess of affairs, watching as he let no fact fall to the ground unattended, I saw I would never have to wonder about what would become of me.

////// //// ////// // ////////

*T*he evening I met Hal Stafford, he was sitting in the rain-scented shade of the maples behind Luther's and Mona's house.

I'd gone over to the house for supper. I'd brought a cherry cobbler with me, the first food I'd actually cooked in what felt like forever. It was made from an easy, cheater's recipe, but I was proud of it and pleased to bring it.

"Oh, that's beautiful," said Mona. "I'll keep it warm in the oven."

As the Staffords' new friend, I felt I might have found a small foothold for myself in the vast flood of my life all around. I was clinging on, determined to scrabble out a tiny patch of goodness for myself, but Mona and Luther were the ones who let me harbor there.

"What are you weaving now?" I said, and she took me to her craft room and showed me. She had a line of tasseled, multi-colored hats and scarves that sold in a little boutique in Edenton. I admired a green and silver scarf. I touched one blue-and-red, child-sized toboggan with the tassels on top like a caterpillar's feelers, turning it over in my hands. I longed to be able to give it to my son.

"Hal stopped by," said Mona, "Luther's brother. I think he may stay for supper, I hope that's all right."

"Of course." I returned the toboggan to its place. This was not my house. They could have anyone to supper that they chose. "I'm going out back to say hello to Maggie a minute."

"Absolutely, go on. Luther's outside feeding everyone, and Hal's back there, too, I guess."

I did not particularly want to talk to Hal, but I went out into the late afternoon. Grass and trees and sky blazed with summer's final splendor. I headed to the goat pen, a place I still expected to reek though it never did. ("That's a myth," Luther had said to me. "Unless it's a male goat rutting, goats really don't have much smell at all," and I'd been astonished to discover how true that was.)

Sunshine smudged and starred all I could see in that direction. I could tell the frolicking, undulating movement of goats, and that someone, undoubtedly Luther, was in the pen with them.

A small stand of reddening maples dipped and rippled at me, and I noticed a man in coveralls seated in a folding chair at the edge of the trees. I decided I should go and introduce myself, since this would have to be Hal, and sure enough, as I neared, squinting through the brightness, I saw that his name had been stitched upon his chest.

He was looking at me, and he rose when I got to him. I was sheltered from the sun by then, and I could see him very well. Like Mona and Luther, he was somewhere about my age, perhaps older. His face held a sharpness—part tenacity, part discernment, part caution—but his eyes seemed old and weary and kind.

"Hello," I said. "Hal, is it? It's good to meet you." I wondered why he was sitting by himself, in proximity to his brother and the goats but not any nearer.

"Likewise." There was a sort of good-natured indolence in Hal's voice, as though no matter what, he had all day. "And you must be the doctor."

Maybe that was true. There had been a lifetime when that was the certainty of me. "Susan," I said. I did not like to call attention to my profession anymore. To do so brought with it a host of questions I wasn't prepared to answer. I'd revealed to Luther and Mona more than most in Clemtown—about my career, my divorce, my leave of absence—but even they did not know about my illness. "Did you just come from work?"

"Yeah," he said. "Hadn't been by here in a while. Thought I should."

"Are you a mechanic, then?"

"Not really. I'm a number of things."

I tried to decide if his answers were meant to be evasive or simply truthful.

"Hi there, Susan," Luther called. "Come on and say a word to Maggie here."

I wondered if he and Hal had been conversing across the distance between pen and trees, if my appearance had put a stop to that.

"You're a goatherd, too?" said Hal to me.

I forced a laugh. "I'm not much of anything at the moment."

The quickness of that reply easing from my mouth stunned me.

"Really?" The crease in Hal's forehead deepened.

We walked toward the fence, and ten, eleven goats pushed and rushed to see us. It was bemusing to see so many attentive animal faces.

The dog, named Daisy, recognized me by now and did not bark.

"Hi, Maggie. Hi, Maggie," I said, amid all the bleating and chaos of goats eating, goats bounding, goats pressing toward the fence.

Maggie looked at me out of her rectangle-pupil eyes and smiled at me with her ever-smiling mouth. I wondered if she might be plotting her next jailbreak.

"You want to hold her?" said Hal.

That possibility had never really occurred to me. It tantalized me now. It daunted me. "Could I?" I turned to Luther.

"Well, of course." Luther stooped and gathered her up, and Maggie didn't struggle much, and Hal met him at the gate to open it. I went that way, too.

When I saw Maggie's slightly scampish face approaching, bleating a little—the goat cradled in Luther's arms—I was consumed with thoughts of Ian and his love for the world's creatures.

Luther handed her to me, and I took her heft, like a human child's, but more awkward to hold against my body—the four legs and the slight scratchiness unfamiliar, the deep-throated bellowing like some unearthly visitation of spirits to a desperate person, kinship and strangeness mingled together in the sounds.

I tried my best to be right there, holding Maggie. She groaned. I didn't think I was doing this right. I felt sure I was not.

She shifted in my grasp, and I tried to grip this goat that did not belong to me, and I could not say why I'd bonded with her—any more than I could really explain my academic pursuit of Anna Maria—but I knew we lived right then a moment of friendship between two penned animals.

Maggie began to flail.

"Careful, there," said Luther, "she may kick you."

"Yes—my brother, the philosopher," said Hal.

"Don't kick me, Maggie." I gave her to Luther again, as Maggie gave me a knowing, smiling look.

Mona's voice warned from the back steps, "There's food in ten minutes."

"We're on our way," Luther shouted, shutting Maggie back behind the gate.

Luther and Mona could still treat in the stuff of ordinary life with each other.

This realization always heartened and saddened me.

"There's a fine thought," said Hal. "Food in ten minutes. Everything we need is ours for the asking."

Already my sense of him was of a disconcerting and haunting personality.

I could tell it would be an interesting evening.

Quite possibly even a welcome one.

///// //// ////// // ////////

Walking from the living room to the kitchen

the kitchen to the bathroom

the bathroom to the living room

I passed many doors I left undisturbed.

The door to my grandparents' room. The door to the bedroom where my father, and then my mother, once slept.

I didn't examine this neglect at first. I'd set up my desk in the living room. I still slept in the living room.

However, it was challenging for me not to come face to face with my younger self around every corner in that house. Especially when Ian came to stay.

And perhaps such encounters were not entirely bad. Maybe I could brave them.

Maybe, I reasoned, if I took a tough look, then what was happening to me now could come into clearer relief.

Because the child who'd lived here and hadn't wanted to had carried a pain I preferred not to behold or share.

Ronald Huffman, my father, left my family when I was seven.

He' d never contacted us again. My mother, Brenda, estranged from her own family, had moved us from Millsborough to Clemtown.

From the time I was old enough to understand, I'd always believed my father's experiences in Vietnam before my birth must have warped and broken him. Compelled him at last to wander off into silence.

As I wandered the house his parents had left me, though, I reconsidered this narrative I'd made. Maybe Ronald Huffman had suffered from more than PTSD.

Maybe I'd inherited my illness from him.

By all accounts a jovial man and a talented artist before he was drafted, my father had come from a family with its share of eccentricities.

Peculiar behaviors are not the same as mental illness. But my reading and study showed me that social stigma had often hindered the understanding of those illnesses historically and rendered them unmentioned. To uncover mental illness in a family's past, you sometimes had to sift through scanty clues.

My aunt, Wanda Huffman, a volatile, vibrant personality, had run off with a man on her eighteenth birthday and sent her parents sporadic postcards for years, visiting them only three times more before her death in an automobile accident.

One cousin, I'd been told, had worked odd jobs and been in and out of jail.

The other was reported to be a semi-recluse.

My papaw, Ben Huffman, an industrious man who met the morning with coffee and the newspaper on a majority of days, nevertheless had some slow starts on occasion, when he stayed abed until after lunch. Other days, he might go for long, solitary walks on his property, not returning home until well past supper.

As for me, when I'd stayed up late many nights in a row— dynamic and unstoppable—to complete schoolwork as a high school student—or when I'd been frustrated by my seeming inability to gain traction on personal projects— feeling enthusiastic one day and disheartened the next—had I exhibited nascent symptoms of bipolar disorder?

It was revelatory to view these old, ordinary moments as maybe meaning something more.

In my early days back in the Huffmans' house, as fall sneaked near, I sometimes ate in the cramped dining room that was more like a hallway between the kitchen and the living room. Alone at that long table.

But when I touched the stove to cook my meals, it was Mamaw touching the stove. I was touching Mamaw. She'd been a Bishop before she married, her existence, her oddities, also part of my inheritance.

An important part. A troubling part.

Mostly I ate in the living room where I, in fact, did most of my living.

The house was quiet except for sounds that originated with me. Outside, the crickets sang, and other animals went about their lives.

In her cabin, Anna Maria Magdalena Muller once sought comfort and instruction from what she knew about the lives of other persecuted, solitary souls, gone before.

The house settled around me. Pieces of my past shifted, began to realign themselves. In the back hall, a sagging door squeaked, trembled wider.

////// //// ////// // ////////

*T*hough I could not yet begin to address the vast muddle of uncertainties in front of me, this one question I could answer.

I decided at last to go to Joy Pridemore's church picnic.

I had no intention of going to her church beforehand.

And I doubted I would make any friends.

In fact, it would be difficult to talk at all—I'd have to censor so much of myself in the process.

But if I went once, I might not have to endure future entreaties.

Or if she brought more invitations, I could maybe miss future events with greater impunity.

The picnic would be in the afternoon, making it easy to get there in time.

And, since I wanted to be able to manage my condition better, here was a chance to practice on these people.

Still I did not face the prospect with much enthusiasm.

I propelled myself out of the house on that mild, sunny afternoon, carrying a bag of potato chips and some onion dip I'd bought in Clemtown.

I'd briefly—very briefly—considered contributing hummus and pita chips from Millsborough or Edenton instead, which I would have preferred.

I'd forced on dress slacks and a blouse slightly nicer than casual, since I assumed everyone else would have on church clothes.

(Actually, in Clemtown, church clothes would mean a dress for a woman, but I was not about to go that far.)

The minute I exited my car, Joy swooped to my side. I was instantly exhausted.

"So glad to see you!" she said.

"It was good of you to invite me," I said.

To my surprise, she divested me of my offerings, handing them into another person's care, and then stayed with me throughout the ordeal, introducing me to the rest of her family, to the preacher, and to everyone. Some remembered me from my past life there, and some I remembered in turn.

"This is Susan Huffman. You remember Susan?" she'd say.

"Hello," I'd say. "It's been a long time."

I had to confess I was glad to be steered about. I believed these people were looking at me with disdain, with hostility— these country people, men and women, young and old, in their Sunday-go-to-meeting clothes—and that their minds were focused entirely on my difference from them.

I tried to chat with them about the weather, about my grandparents, about long-ago school days, and I could tell by some of their expressions I was not managing very well. I was curt and brusque today, more so than I'd meant.

Or worse, maybe I'd been curt and brusque all my life, and only now was I beginning to notice.

Or. Maybe I was doing all right. Maybe my ability to read people's reactions was entirely compromised that day, and they were thinking no such thing.

Joy kept smiling and talking and helping. I could not explain why she wanted me there.

Looking at the people with their faces of clay, I tried to feel tender towards them. I tried to recognize that each of them perhaps carried something secret, the way I carried my bipolar disorder. That each of us was wounded and limited and frail.

I was not spectacularly successful.

As Joy walked me through the gauntlet, as I dished food onto my plate—ham and green beans, mashed potatoes with no gravy—as I watched women talking, men talking, spouses talking, I caught myself feeling over and over like a beggar. I who had once been a hostess. I settled at a table with the Pridemores, where the oldest child, a daughter, began to confide in me how she hated algebra homework, and I ate and sought to respond at the right times and in the right ways. Little children laughed and chased one another as the shadows imperceptibly began to lengthen.

/////// ///// /////// // ////////

One morning I recognized that I had to find something purposeful to do.

I could only watch so much daytime television.

I'd cleaned. I'd read on the porch.

I'd followed Papaw's example and took walks across the fields. The land smelled gold and spicy. The view of mountains from one spot near the edge of the woods did not take my breath—it infused me with breath. It gave me a moment of hope.

One day, I vowed, I would get out of here.

But here I was in the meantime.

So I drove to the Clemtown Public Library, still located in the brick basement of the town hall. I was not sure what I had in mind. All I knew was that the library had proved to be a lifeline for me in the years I'd lived here before. Maybe it could be so again.

An aged matriarch of a librarian had worked in it once, Mrs. McGhee, who did not say much except to chide loud children. But she took a liking to me, I will never know why, and pointed me to books by Elizabeth George Speare and Scott O'Dell, slipped me lollipops as I left. Her terse tutelage had helped me to imagine other settings than mine, to believe I could even inhabit them, if I desired.

Now I walked into the small room, cold and hushed, which housed adult circulation and reference as it had all those years ago. The walls were the same beige. The floor was the same brown. It still smelled like old paper in there. A couple of computers, not here before, but that was the only difference I could see.

In the past, I'd always headed on through to the far door and the children's department, Mrs. McGhee's old domain. Today I stayed in the main room.

Behind the adult circulation desk an old man sat. I was the only other person in the place.

I went toward the desk.

"Hello," said the man. His face was malleable with wrinkles, and he had a powdery voice, but his eyes were sprightly. "Can I help you, miss?"

I decided to overlook the *miss*. "Do you all ever need volunteers?"

He seemed startled. "Volunteers?"

I nodded. "People to help shelve books. Or dust the shelves. Something quiet. I could come one day a week for a few hours."

I could surely manage that.

He stared. His eyebrows climbed. "Why, that would be wonderful."

"Great," I said. "I'm Susan Huffman, and I can come whichever day is best for you."

"Pete Smith," he said, and his lips moved back in a tremulous smile. "So you're little Susie Huffman, are you? You probably don't remember me, but I remember you. Your mamaw and papaw brought you to church and all. I taught your daddy in high school."

"Really?" I said, although it would make no sense for him to make that up.

"Oh, yes, I was the art teacher then. That's been a few years." He gave a dry and stretchy laugh.

I wondered what my father had been in this man's class, when all Ronald Huffman would have had in view was to hone his talent, find his place among his peers, get each semester put by. "It's nice to meet you, Mr. Smith."

"Oh, you can call me Pete. Everybody does. If you got a minute, you want me to show you how things do around here?'

I had any number of minutes. "Yes, please." Here was the prospect of learning from a man who'd taught my father, a father I'd barely known, and I was intrigued.

"All right." Pete pushed back his chair and got gingerly down. "Right this way."

I believed this meant I'd come to the right place.

A place I could maybe matter in.

///// //// ///// // ///////

In the cooling afternoon, Charles and Nate and I were standing on my front porch and talking—they'd dropped by to visit and were about to leave—when Hal's pickup turned into the driveway.

This staggered me.

Soon I would be headed out to Luther's and Mona's for dinner. And Hal, I'd known, would come there to dinner, too.

What I hadn't known, however, was that Hal was first coming here.

The truck settled to a stop. I exchanged goodbyes with my friends.

As Charles and Nate headed down the walk, Hal walked up from the driveway. The men all spoke and nodded as they passed each other.

But I saw Hal giving them a lingering, sidelong glance.

Charles and Nate were holding hands.

Great, I thought. So Luther's brother is a philistine.

"Hello, Hal," I said. "Fancy seeing you here."

There was something unsettling about him always. "I'm here to pick you up."

"Oh," I said. "Okay."

Though Hal's voice was easygoing, and his eyes were mild, he carried a palpable intensity. Had a way of lurking even as he stood in plain sight.

I said, "Let me get my purse and sweater and the lemon potatoes." I didn't want to offend Luther's brother, but I had legs, and I had a car, and I hadn't known I was to be the recipient of this service.

I went for my things. When I came out, I was locking the door and balancing the dish of baked, herbed, and lemony potatoes.

"I can take that," Hal said.

"Thanks," I said, "I've got it." I heard the lock thunk.

We walked to his truck in silence. I tried to decide what was best for me to say.

"You know," said Hal, "I didn't even think about bringing anything." He got into the truck, and leaned and unlocked my door. "I just got off work," he went on, as I opened it, "but I suppose I should have. Brought something." He indicated me with his chin. "That makes you a lot better than me, Doctor, thinking about things like that."

I hoped I wasn't being courted. Or stalked.

I became more leery than ever about the impending ride.

"I doubt it." I climbed in. "Making this just gave me something to do. Since I'm not working at the moment, and I'm sorting some personal problems out."

When I shut the door, the cab felt very tight.

"Your judge, you mean," Hal started the truck. "That's what Luther said."

The dish full of food was balanced in my lap, and the truck was moving. I had to be there. "So, you know I'm in the midst of a divorce, then." I hoped I was being tactful, underscoring things gently. "And Samuel and I are having a custody dispute."

"No, I didn't know that," said Hal. "About custody."

The truck lurched and rocked and churned gravel, headed toward the highway.

"Yes, I have an all-but-three-year-old. So, you see, my life is plenty complicated."

"It sure looks that way, yes."

"Well," I said, ready and afraid to speak, "I've got more than I can really manage right now, Hal, and I want you to understand, I want to be very clear about this. It's probably better if I don't have a lot of extra—entanglements."

He'd been about to turn into the road. He applied the brakes instead. "What is that supposed to mean?"

I took a breath for clarity and courage. "It means—"

"I know damn well what it means," he said. "Listen to yourself. Almighty Dr. Susan Huffman, have you got some nerve. Hellfire. Where do you think you come by the right to decide I have any interest in you whatsoever?—besides the fact that you're my brother's neighbor, and that would make you a friend to me?"

He glared. The truck idled.

I'd forgotten all my words.

"I'm—sorry," I stammered. "I didn't understand—why the ride—"

"I was just driving by." He looked at the windshield. "I was just being friendly."

I remembered giving the homeless man a lift in my car.

I was mortified. In every way possible.

"I ought to make you walk," he said. "I ought to make you get out right here."

I reached for the seat belt latch, my face full of nuclear fallout. *Please forgive my mistake*, I wanted to say, I began to say.

"No. I mean. . . ." He pushed his hand through the air, a gesture like frustration, defeat. "Excuse my language, all of it. That was too strong of me."

I looked at the aluminum foil that covered my potatoes. "I've said worse. Heard worse." I was shaking my head. "Please forgive my mistake, Hal."

"No, it's just, I have this bipolar," he said.

It was now my turn to stare.

"It's a condition," he said, like this was something he felt I needed to know. "The way diabetes is or high blood pressure— they don't like you to say *I am bipolar* anymore, like you're the same thing as your brain chemistry—but—I don't always mean to be that rude. I can be too forceful. I apologize for that."

I was still staring. "You?"

For his strangeness was illuminated for me all at once, that contradictory sense I had of him reconciled.

Hal lobbed me a questioning look.

"That's," I said, "what I have."

Something opened in his face, behind his eyes.

"That's what happened to me," I said.

He frowned. "That would make him a pitiful excuse for a man, wouldn't it?"

I shifted my eyes to the window and the side mirror, taking in the stretch of driveway behind us, the towering evergreens. "Samuel's Samuel. And I really don't want to talk about him."

"No. Sorry. Of course not."

My calf itched. "Can we start this over?"

Hal's truck creaked forward. Paused. "Sure." Pulled into the highway.

"It was thoughtful of you to come and collect me, Hal," I said, looking out still. "Thank you."

"We're headed the same way. Plus I got to meet your friends."

In my leg, the prickling eased. "I thought you seemed uncomfortable with them."

"No," he said like a shrug. "If I was nosy, I didn't mean to be. It's not like I see that every day. But I didn't mean a thing by it. Everybody's got a right to do how they want, I guess."

He didn't phrase his insight the way I would have preferred, but I decided to let it go.

The field of early autumn rolled by my window, and my neighbors' house came into view.

///// //// ///// // ///////

Unlike his brother, who commuted to work at the chemical plant in Millsborough five days a week, Hal worked odd jobs around Clemtown. He cleaned churches and mowed lawns. He washed cars and processed donations at the thrift store, and he performed all duties while wearing those coveralls bearing his name.

For several years, I learned, Hal had stocked shelves at the sad little community grocery, located at the solitary gas station (where Roberta now worked), until the son of the owners lost a good job in Windy Grove and returned home needing employment. Hal had also cleaned the elementary school and the town hall until a contractor was retained for that purpose.

Hal lived near the abandoned train depot in an ancient house that had been converted into a duplex. He'd lived with a string of marginalized or disreputable women over the years—he'd been shot by one woman, for example, and robbed by another—but never, to anyone's knowledge, been married.

Currently, Hal lived alone except for a canary named Barry.

Though I remembered Hal's and Luther's grandparents, I could not come up with any reliable childhood memory of Hal or Luther themselves, visiting Clemtown. Hal had only ended up a resident after quitting school and drifting around East Tennessee, and Luther and Mona had moved here several years after.

To be closer to Hal.

I imagined Hal at home. He lived in two rooms. He had no television, only a radio. He read day-old newspapers given him by the community grocery, and he'd read most of the books in the Clemtown library. He ate peanut butter and jelly sandwiches and tomato soup and drank buttermilk and let Barry the canary out of his cage twice a day to fly to the top of a non-functioning grandfather clock and sing in place of the clock chimes.

What details I could not get from Luther and Mona or others, I made up myself.

Once a month, Hal helped a team of volunteers serve hot breakfast out of a church kitchen to Clemtown residents who were down on their luck. I marveled when I first found that out, since I would have thought him abundantly qualified to be on the receiving end of such a serving line.

Because of my own domestic situation, unless we met in social settings with other people present, I avoided Hal Stafford. I knew that any perceived relationship with him beyond the barest courtesy acquaintance—he was, after all, my neighbor's brother—would be ample pretext for Samuel to seek to keep Ian away from me.

I never took Ian to Luther's and Mona's if Hal would be there.

And Hal never came if Ian was with me.

///// //// ///// // ///////

*N*owadays, Ian and I look like this:

In the midst of his playing on the hardwood floor, he glances up at me.

We've eaten homemade macaroni and cheese, green peas, and garlic bread. We've blown soap bubbles on the front porch. We've watched *101 Dalmatians* and *The Lion King* on my new DVD player. We've devoured picture books checked out from the Clemtown library, where I now have a legitimate library card.

"Mommy?" he says.

"Yes, baby?"

We have an invitation to the Staffords' for lunch tomorrow and time with Maggie.

"I want me go home," Ian says.

His face is not sad, only a little weary, at a loss.

His voice is not tearful, but confiding and honest.

And in that moment, I can't say what I should say.

That this is Mommy's home now, and it's his home, too. That he is always, always welcome here.

"I know," I say instead. He's within reach of my hand, and I lay it against his cheek. For I share his wish to erase everything that has changed, to be in a place of wholeness, where I am whole. "Me, too."

////// //// ////// // ////////

That fall I continued to visit my psychiatrist, who continued to tweak my medications.

I also kept going to sessions with Annika.

In her presence, it was easier for me to see my situation as it was, regardless of the pain, regardless of the outcome.

My situation had not changed in the slightest. I was the one undergoing the change.

////// //// ////// // ////////

I was shelving books at the Clemtown library one afternoon, sore with depression, when I creaked my head around, and there came Hal Stafford in his coveralls lugging a bag of trash out of the women's restroom.

What did I feel, seeing him?

He saw me in nearly the same moment. He set the trash bag down and came over.

He made me uncomfortable, always, and yet the sight of him lent an odd kind of comfort. He was the one person in Clemtown who knew me, knew the truth of me. It was a relief not to have to pretend something different.

"Well, if it isn't the doctor." Hal waited to speak until he was nearly at my elbow, though few patrons were in the building. "Should have known you'd be investigating the library. You doing all right?" He didn't smile, but his old, kind, weary eyes lightened, perhaps. He was a little closer to me than I would have liked, and he smelled of work.

"More or less." I was alive. I could move. "More like less. And you?"

A frown began spreading through his eyes. "Got a new job, as you can see, it'll do." He shrugged as he said this, his commentary on the job. "So. What's less?"

"You know. The usual. Everything."

The frown reached his face. He glanced around and lowered his voice still more. "Listen, Doctor, I'll tell you what's really helped me."

I wasn't sure I wanted to know.

"There's a support group that meets twice a month in Millsborough," he said. "It's for people with depression and bipolar disorder."

I'd begun wincing inside my chest as soon as he uttered the words, *support group.* "I don't know."

"The fellow who moderates is a trained psych nurse," Hal said, "so he's a professional. The rest of us just have life experience to offer." He said this last like it was some bad joke.

I rocked a step back, closer to the returned books cart. I realized I was folding my arms. "That sounds like a good thing, but I'm not sure if I want to sit in a room full of"—I began to say *crazy people*—"strangers and talk about my life." I imagined a room full of people twitching, rolling their eyes about, gnashing their teeth, incoherent, terrifying. I had a hard time imagining myself in their company, even less—however nominally—as one of them.

"Sure," said Hal, "takes some getting used to, hard to say if it's for you." He shuffled back a step or two as well. "All I can say is, it absolutely changed my life. No question about that, for me."

His endorsement gave me pause. I wondered what I was afraid of.

Then he mentioned that the group met in a church basement, and I knew there was no way, no way, I was going anywhere near that place.

Religion meant insanity to me now.

"If you ever change your mind," he said.

"I'll think about it."

I expressed some proper thanks, and that ended the subject under discussion. Hal went back to his job, and I returned to mine, parting books, lifting books, shifting books, withdrawing to numbness, somewhere I longed to be.

As I drove home that evening, the light was slowly failing.

Barns I'd known were crumbling to ruin against the reddening hills. Or they'd been pulled down, and trailer parks, subdivisions for commuters, now occupied the spaces. Land grew organic produce and heirloom vegetables for farmers' markets in Edenton and Millsborough.

It was all so unlike what Clemtown was, what I'd remembered. How could I be this thunderstruck to lose what I'd never wanted. The tobacco fields were no more.

///// //// ///// // ///////

On an autumn afternoon, I lug my dulcimer case out, I don't know why.

I take up the instrument and lay it across my lap.

This is my dulcimer still. It is still mine.

Turning the pegs, I tune the strings to each other. I listen as I pluck them, storing the notes in my mind, comparing them.

I wrangle my favorite pick from the bag that holds my capo, too. I strum the strings, deciding what I will play.

I choose a fast fiddle tune. My fingers fumble, and I stop and start the music, working through the piece.

When I get to the end, I begin over.

I don't mess up as much this time.

I play it again. I try to enjoy the feel of my fingers on the strings, the tension in my arms and hands.

I am pleased to make this music, bring it into this house, where even the few small rooms are too big for me.

As I play

I try not to hear Lorraine and her marvelous banjo

I try not to hear the evident giftedness in her music
I try to will myself into contentment with my middling talent.

I refuse to see the scope of my present life as Lorraine Davis's leavings.

As I play my dulcimer on that robust and heady autumn afternoon, I try to imagine I have never known anyone named Anna Maria Magdalena Muller to have ever lived.

///// //// ///// // ///////

I was coming out of the post office with my book of stamps one day, when I noticed Joy Pridemore exiting the library, in the building next door.

It seemed that the library connected with more people than I'd thought.

We met in the parking lot.

"Why, hello there, Susan!" She was carrying two books, which looked to be a devotional and a chaste-looking romance. "You still getting on all right?"

"Yes, thanks. How are things with you?" I tried not to let our differing tastes in reading material distract me from the conversation.

"Pretty good, we're all in good health, which is such a blessing!"

"Is your daughter still hating algebra?" It was something light to say. I'd appreciated my conversation with the girl at the picnic.

"She is," said Joy, laughing a little, "but she works at it, and she's going to have a B this time, which is good. But I'll tell you, I don't know what I'm going to do with that boy of mine."

She continued with her slightly laughing voice, like she'd named a trifling trouble, but I saw otherwise in her eyes.

"Elijah's never been the student Rachel is," Joy said, "but this year he just seems to struggle, I don't know why. If he wants to do anything with his life, he's got to apply himself." She seemed to draw inward, to be addressing herself and Elijah almost as much as me. "He needs to know his American history, I tell him, I think that's real important to know what this country is about. It's like he's given up trying. I can't get him to take it seriously."

I remembered Elijah from the picnic. About ten years old, quiet, with downcast eyes.

I wondered what Ian would be at ten.

"Joy," I heard myself saying, "that's what I studied in school." I did not say I had a doctorate in history, I did not say that American history was my career, my *area of expertise.* "If you need a tutor, I could try spending some time with him on his lessons."

Her whole face went wide. "Really? Would you? Oh! I had no idea. I mean, I knew you were always the smart one, but. . . ." Her eyes shimmered with water. "Oh! This is wonderful! This is perfect!"

This was embarrassing, to have done nothing to merit her effusiveness. I shifted my pocketbook. "I can't promise my help will change anything, but I'll certainly do my best." Though it would be a change, teaching again.

"Oh! I know you will, and I'm sure it will help. Let me go home and talk to Elijah."

I thought of Lindsey and her unique and terrible paper. I didn't know if my understanding of *what this country was about* squared with Lindsey's or not, with Joy's or not. Probably not. But I absolutely believed in the importance of knowing its past.

Joy was unlocking the door of her car. "I'd been praying to know what to do," she said, "and there you were, next door to me the whole time."

She closed her car door, and I got in and shut mine. I didn't know why I had offered to help, but also I did. And it certainly had nothing to do with her prayer.

I had a son, too.

///// //// ///// // ////////

*F*or Ian's third birthday, in late October, I am at my old house.

Samuel's house, now.

A place where all traces of me have been removed.

A place we all must pretend I never was.

Meredith is the one who answers the door and lets me into my house.

"I can take your jacket," she offers, uncertainly.

"Thanks, I know where the coat closet is," I say.

When I enter the living room, three of the daycare mothers greet me with an eager enthusiasm that is meant, no doubt, to mask their discomfort as well as mine.

Hannah Ellison, Samuel's mother—apparently ferried from the nursing home for the day—dozes in the recliner.

Samuel himself is able to look at me from across the room as if I'm a mere rumor, unconfirmed before his face until now.

"Susan," he says to acknowledge me.

I'm able to walk farther in without collapsing. I am able also to say his name.

It looks like I never once cooked there, showered there, slept there.

Much less that I did those things for nearly four years there, and that I was happy to be there when I was.

Ian is playing with a toy barnyard and its plastic farm animals with his friends and ignores me longer than I would have believed possible. Lammykin, sprawled in the floor, stares where I stand.

Lorraine, most mercifully, is not in attendance.

"Mommy," says Ian.

He races over, and I lean to give him his present, which holds a storybook of Aesop's fables and a stuffed lion, but Samuel says my name again, this time like I'm not quick enough to catch on.

So I have to look at my husband.

"We're going to open the gifts after the cake," he says.

Before I can object or concur, Meredith takes the present from me to put on a table with the other wrapped boxes there.

"Mommy, looky," says Ian. He takes my hand and tugs me, and I let him lead me to the toy barnyard, where the three other children swarm around me also. "See me farm? I'm Farmer Dell."

"Wow, you're the farmer in the dell, huh?" I say.

"Yeah, I'm Farmer Dell. Mommy, looky," Ian says again. He goes running to another corner of the room—"Ian, don't run," Samuel says—and comes back hefting a large and colorful Noah's ark in both arms. "See me ark? I got *all* the animals."

"Boy, I bet you do," I say, kneeling. "Can you show me?"

Ian sets the ark down and starts pulling out pairs of creatures.

"Were you thinking of putting those other toys of yours away first?" says Samuel.

Ian ignores his father now. "See sheep? And horseys? And bears? And birdies?" He names each pair for me, as his friends crowd close.

"My goodness, you know every one of your animals," I say.

"Uh-huh. Lorraine told me them. She give me ark. Told me story."

So. There it was.

Lorraine is not in the room, not in the house. But she isn't absent from our festivities. She is very much there.

I watch Ian march his creatures back into the ark. Before the other mothers and Meredith, Ian's grandmother and my husband, in the presence of the unseen interloper who has taken my domain, there is nowhere else in the room I can look right then.

"She certainly knows what you like," I tell Ian.

Whereas I no longer know if what I have chosen is the best present for my son.

But I do know this—Lorraine's gift has not been forced to wait its turn on the table with the others.

///// //// ///// // //////

*I*n January—not even a year ago—when Mike and Lorraine Davis had only newly come into Samuel's life and not yet into mine—before I'd ever had the least notion I could *declare new ways* or see floating tables in my study—only earlier that very same year, it had snowed four or five inches overnight.

The next day, the courts were closed. The college was closed. Samuel, Ian, and I were home together.

We had our usual weekends, of course. But this was something different. Unexpected.

We'd risen early to figure out from the news what our day might look like. Once it was evident we were marooned—a tantalizing prospect—I cooked us pancakes and fried some ham steaks originally intended to be served with asparagus and Hollandaise that weekend. Samuel laid a fire in the fireplace and carted the highchair into the living room. Ian ate his breakfast I'd slathered with honey—"Yay, me eat!" he proclaimed when presented with his meal—and Samuel and I ate ours with maple syrup on TV trays. All in pajamas still, we watched *Sesame Street* while we ate.

As the day went on, we built towers of blocks together, and Ian gleefully knocked them down. We read stories. We played hide-and-seek, with either Samuel or me counting for Ian and helping him locate the hidden parent, or one of us hiding with Ian until found. Hiding or seeking, Ian always shrieked with laughter at the moment of discovery, which was the best part, and made my husband smile. "Do again!" Ian would say. "Do again!" When we came to the end of the hide-and-seek part of our day, Samuel scooped up our laugh-howling child and kissed him and then kissed me. I was very happy, too.

We had peanut butter sandwiches for lunch, eating in the living room again. I put honey on Ian's and sliced banana on Samuel's and mine. When Ian went down for his nap, neither Samuel nor I went to our respective studies to work. We stood at the living room window awhile with some decaf coffee and watched the snow fall. We sat on the couch and napped a little ourselves and talked about work—a thing Samuel rarely did— and about where we might go on vacation with Ian. The fire popped and hissed as though it, too, had things to say. I let all the words and the time soak deep into me.

I decided to make a meatloaf for supper. While I cooked, Samuel gave Ian his bath and some clean pajamas, and later I listened to them reading and talking in the living room. It sounded like Ian was covering Giant up with a pillow or a blanket and then saying, "Found you!" Samuel would say, "Well, what do you know," and I chimed in a time or two with, "Did you find Giant again?"

There wasn't any Lammykin then for him to find.

After meatloaf and mashed potatoes and peas and carrots, we turned the lights out in the living room, and the fire glowed, and the house smelled fantastic, like it had been thoroughly cooked in and played in and lived in. We put on one of Ian's cartoons, and we let him fall asleep between us there on the couch, before we carried him up to his room.

Tomorrow would be Saturday. The road would be plowed, and the snow would be gone before that weekend's end. But that night, Samuel and I stood watching Ian sleep, with our arms around each other, with a great, wide place inside my chest that I thought could have no end, and my eyes got a little wet as I realized I was looking ahead at the days we would have. If that snowy day in any way resembled the smallest part of what lay in store, I'd wanted them all.

///// //// ///// // ////////

*I*n the night, I heard the Staffords' dog, Daisy, barking in my dreams.

The sound didn't rouse me. It blended with my sleep somehow.

But the crack of a gun echoing over November fields stunned me awake.

Bewildered, I cast around in the dark. I wasn't sure what I'd heard, not then.

I rustled up from the couch. My bare feet cold on the living room floor, I stood in the shadows, listening for what I should do.

Daisy kept barking. I heard no more shots.

Probably I shouldn't go out onto the porch, I thought.

Yet that is exactly what I did.

First, however, I tied on my robe and grabbed my keys.

In the hard, earth-scented, country dark, I peered across the pasture toward the Staffords' and saw a light—flashlight? lantern?—bobbing around behind the house. In the vicinity of the stand of maples.

I did not know what was happening. I thought of several possibilities.

I dashed back into the house and snatched up the phone. I called Luther and Mona.

The phone rang several times.

Just as I began to hang up and dial 911, the line clicked on, and Mona said, "Hello?"

"Mona, it's Susan." The Staffords did not have caller ID. "You've got somebody in your back yard. Is everything all right?"

"Oh, Susan, we've lost one of the goats." I heard tears breaking up Mona's voice, blurring her words. "Luther's out back, checking. But we're pretty sure it's Maggie."

"Maggie?" My brain feebly scrabbled to catch up to what she'd said. Latch onto something.

All I could get was a memory of the little creature trotting into my yard.

"A coyote got her," Mona was saying. "That's what we think, and we think it's been—hit—gone off to live or die. Which I hate to consider either way. But a goat is missing from the pen, and—there's a half-eaten carcass out past the trees."

I could have gone a long time without that image in my head. My whole life, in fact.

"I guess she got out again," Mona said.

I clung to the receiver. "How perfectly awful."

"Yes, it is," Mona said, crying softly. "Would you—want to come over? Of course we're up. I know you were fond of her."

How foolish to be so lost over the death of somebody else's animal. "I don't think I can," I said. "But please tell Luther you all are welcome to bury her on my property."

Not that the Staffords didn't have plenty of places to put her.

But, "I will," said Mona.

There was a certain cedar tree I was thinking of, down by the pond.

"She never could stay put," I said. "That was endearing to me."

There was no more sleeping to be done that night.

Throughout the morning, when I least expected or wanted to, I kept seeing the image of a bloody, mangled animal, bone and skin, entrails and hair, smeared and rotting upon the ground.

And I kept getting the twisting, sickening feeling that this creature had been mistaken for me.

Late that afternoon, Luther brought Hal and a shovel and Maggie's body wrapped in burlap and old bedsheets. Mona did not come.

I was not sure that I wanted Hal there.

We went to the pond and the tree. At first Luther had balked. "This could foul the water," he said.

"I've concluded," I said, "that any water I might have is poisoned already. Everything else of mine is. I don't care."

Neither Hal nor Luther had anything to say to that.

So Maggie was buried there. It was a hard job, and I wished I could have been more of a help. As it was, I stood there and watched them labor. I watched the muddy water and the rocks, the cedars and the sky.

When the hole in the earth was filled once more, it was a certainty that Maggie was no longer in the world.

"You want me to say something?" Hal said.

He was asking if he ought to give a funeral service. Offer prayers for Maggie.

"I'd prefer it if you didn't," I said.

He wiped his hands on the legs of his coveralls. "That's all right, too."

We went back to the house. I gave them some cold water—the remark about my water's poison hovering like a revenant over the act—and the men left soon after.

I returned to the pond.

I watched the trees some more. I watched the water.

The sun was falling to earth. It would land somewhere far beyond the Staffords' house, beyond the mountains.

And there I was.

With absolutely no next that I could see.

I stood there, hurting and so hollow.

My body all but eradicated. My core exposed, battered nearly to nothing.

The wind strove against me. Stirred the grass. Ruffled the water.

The world turning cold.

I tried not to confront the obvious: I could wade into the pond.

Mamaw had waded into water once.

Hulda Bishop, whoever she might have been, had long ago slipped into that cold creek. The tug of water rising to her hips. Her footing lost, her body pushed under. Like a drowning, like a burial.

The pond in the twilight.

And yet she'd been righted. Tipped up out of it, by someone's hands. Set on her feet once more so she could seek the shore.

I saw her swim-striving in white, her dress heavy with the water's pull.

I saw her clambering, reaching, being hauled up the bank.

Even if she'd been as deluded about her experience as I'd been about mine.

I'd had moments, too, despite everything, where I'd found myself on firm ground. Past all explanation or understanding.

God, I did not say, *why would you ever ask me to believe that you exist when you are nothing but my sickness.*

God, oh, God, I wanted there to be a God there.

The sky was awash with red and gold in the west. Darkness spilled from the east.

As the landscape slowly disappeared about me, here was what was left, not swallowed away, this was what I knew:

I was still standing.

After all the injustice visited on me, all I'd endured, I was still there.

///// //// ///// // //////

I turned on the light in the living room.

I turned on the light in the kitchen. The dining room.

I picked up one of the dining table chairs and lugged it from the room.

I carried the chair down the hall.

I turned on the light in the hall.

I carried the chair to the bedroom that had once been my father's.

In that room, too, I turned on the light.

I didn't look at anything long. Except the closet.

Only the closet.

I opened the closet door and set the chair at the entrance.

I grasped the cord to the closet light and tugged.

There was abruptly light.

I didn't glance at the ugly doll at the back of the close, stark closet.

Instead I climbed into the chair.

Until I stood in the chair.

Reaching to the back of the shelf in the closet, I snagged and dragged my notebook to the edge.

Here was a new thing I could try.

I could convert this notebook of mine into a record of my struggle with my illness. A record of learning and coping.

Maybe, one day, a record of thriving.

A way to share my discoveries with others.

To declare to skeptics and to sufferers alike that it is possible to survive.

Because what I was becoming was not yet known.

Stretched there with my fingers on the notebook's cover, I dithered, I debated, then determined I would leave the Bible where it was. For now.

I drew the notebook down.

///// //// ////// // ////////

After a late afternoon appointment with Annika, I called Nell to see if I could come by awhile, since I was in Edenton and hadn't seen in her in much too long. She insisted on meeting me instead and taking me to supper.

I was grateful for the offer. I hadn't eaten since breakfast, and I was starving. "How would Nethermore be?" I said. "I love their pizza."

"You're sure that's where you want to go?" said Nell.

Samuel had introduced me to the place when we were dating.

"Am I going to let Samuel bleed all the happiness from my life?" I said.

So Nethermore it was.

The eatery was an odd, unprepossessing, out-of-the-way place on a narrow back street, almost an alley. Samuel did not, in general, make a habit of frequenting restaurants like it, but their food was excellent, and the service was, too, so we'd gone there together often. The rooms were snug and dim, and the booths were deep.

Nell and I studied our menus. I wanted a grilled chicken and mushroom pizza so I could take leftovers back to Clemtown, a reminder to me that the rest of the world was out there still.

"I think I'll have the pesto spaghetti," said Nell.

Our waiter didn't recognize me at first. "You look so different," he said.

I'd gained twenty pounds and was wearing jeans and a sweatshirt.

Also—I was not with the chancellor.

"It's not my best hair day," I said.

The restaurant was starting to get busy. The waiter brought bread and our salads. More people arrived.

"I've got to do something about my appearance," I said. I was not accustomed to the slovenly, sluggish woman who wore my clothes in those days.

"You will," said Nell. "Be patient with yourself. You have to heal."

I was afraid there would be no end to that endeavor.

The food came. I served myself a slice of pizza. Nell reached for the shaker of parmesan cheese.

"Susan," said Nell.

But I was already seeing what she saw.

The host was seating Chancellor Ellison and Lorraine Davis at the booth directly across from us.

Nell said nothing. I said nothing.

The two of them settled into their seats and reflected on their menus as the host left. Through the shadows, I sat and watched them.

I tried not to want to be across the room.

Lorraine and Samuel returned their menus to the table. They looked at one another. They looked at no one else, saw no one, did not see me at all.

He talked to her. She smiled her homespun smile and leaned towards him.

I felt the piercing certainty of finitude.

I let the pizza lie on my plate.

Once the waitress collected their orders and their menus and departed, Samuel seemed to gather himself as if to rise.

Only then did Samuel's eyes meet with mine.

He knew who I was.

If he had been dead in that moment, though, the man could not have been more distant from me.

I heard Nell's swift hiss of breath.

The chancellor absorbed Nell's presence, too. In those apprehending eyes of his. That careful face.

I saw Lorraine seeing us. Her eyes impossibly ardent.

I saw it all.

I perceived Samuel evaluating our situation from every angle. Including mine.

For he could keep our divorce proceedings out of court if he did that.

If he agreed to my custody demands and settled in mediation.

Which he might prefer to do now.

He was an elected official, after all, in East Tennessee.

A prominent man. A still-married man.

Seeing my husband at Nethermore, though—with the Lady of the *Giantkillers*, no less—felt like the very farthest thing from victory I could ever attain.

///// //// ///// // ////////

And so my mad imaginings have proven true.

Did God warn me? Was there a God to warn me?

Or was it my paranoia, my psychosis, that drove my husband into her fervent, waiting, sympathetic arms?

Annika helps me to see what matters is to accept the facts—of my illness, my broken marriage, the presence of Lorraine in Ian's life. That is difficult enough. To wrestle with the rest is waste.

I can believe that life is filled with ambiguity and happenstance. Anna Maria, too, mused on the congruities and incongruities of her own life, in passages such as this one:

"I have dwelled in the shadow of His love and of His revelations until the whole of my life has darkened, and yet His commands give me light enough. In that light is a blaze of beauty and of truth that kindles all I touch. How can my life be dark beneath that glory light?"   —*Anna Maria Magdalena Muller*

Though her visions may have been delusion, her sufferings were real. I am able to understand and to honor perseverance in anyone who endures when their whole world goes dark.

Though I have no glory light left to shine for me.

And so. I'm not quite ready for the future, I'm afraid, but it's coming for me, all the same.

When the future and I are ready together, I hope to return to my work at the college. But I know, despite my wishes, my way ahead must be different now, whether I return or not.

Alongside the old work, I'd like to foster the impetus to fashion something new.

Can I embrace the form this newness will take?

I have considered

A historical lecture series

A book club for girls

Enrichment offerings for the mothers of small children

Or career counseling sessions for women

Or something else

At the Clemtown library

Or anywhere.

(Perhaps Dr. Rickwell might support my project. Contribute her time.)

And I could call this unknown venture, "Maggie's Hometown Studies."

In memory of Anna Maria Magdalena Muller.

And one little goat.

/////// //// ////// // ////////

On a day in a stretch of November, after Samuel collects Ian from my house, and they leave together—when I am alone once more, and the quiet is so utter I hear the inexorable second hand of the clock fastidiously taking its time—in that hour is when I feel something go firm and translucent inside me, and I decide.

I put on jeans and a sweater and a pair of brown leather heels.

My Kaspar suit no longer fits as well as I would like.

I make up my face for the first time in weeks.

I grab my pocketbook and a jacket.

I leave the house, too.

It is coming on evening. The year is heading to winter so very fast.

I drive to Millsborough. The same road that my son and my husband are on.

But they will turn right at one traffic light, and I will turn right at another.

I know what my destination is. Still I've never gone here before.

As the world darkens, the little city manufactures its own lights in abundance, street lights and traffic lights, the signs of business, the headlights of vehicles. I'd forgotten how much glass existed here, and how panes of glass can gleam like rivers in the night.

I'll be late. I am never late to anything.

My hands clammy on the steering wheel, I turn off the road and into the parking lot of an unfamiliar church.

There are more cars here than I would've thought.

This is where Hal said the meeting would be.

I stop the car and get out. I wander through the parking lot looking for a likely entrance into the building.

The wind throws my hair into my eyes.

I don't want to be here. I don't want to be in a place with a steeple and a room full of unbalanced, dangerous people.

But I want to be well. If it is possible for me.

I will do whatever I can to make that come true.

I try a door that looks promising, and it opens.

A few steps in, I find stairs leading down.

I take the stairs, and as I reach the bottom, I hear voices.

A door sits ajar to my right. In that room is where the people are.

I resist the urge to go back upstairs. I walk to the door and push it wider.

All the faces in the room look where I stand. The talking stops.

It's been a while since I stood in front of a room of people.

"Excuse me," I say. "Is this the bipolar support group meeting?"

I see a circle of chairs and a dry erase board and all those faces.

And there is Hal's face. His expression just then shifting, but from what to what, I cannot say.

"Yes, it is," says a man in scrubs. "Come on in."

And I do. "I apologize for being late," I say to the whole room. "I didn't know if I was coming or not."

"You're just fine," says the man in scrubs. "Have a seat and join us."

There's an empty chair in Hal's vicinity. About five seats away from where he sits. I take that one.

I'm rather relieved I can't sit closer.

The man in scrubs turns back toward a woman seated across the circle from him, and says, "You said you're still having disagreements with your mother-in-law?"

The woman, whose stick-on nametag says she's *Sondra*, nods.

I realize everyone wears a nametag but me.

"She disrespects me every chance she gets," says Sondra and elaborates.

It's hard to follow her story, coming in halfway. I try to listen, but I'm also trying to absorb my surroundings. The room has small windows high on two walls. The walls are dark, and the floor is dark, but the overhead light is very bright. A long table on one wall has bowls of snacks—popcorn and pretzels and M&Ms—and a stack of paper plates. There are also cans of soda, all of the choices caffeine-free.

On the table, too, I see papers and pamphlets. That may be where the name tags are.

But above the table hangs a picture of Jesus. His sad and solemn face. His big, dark eyes looking out at us all.

Which makes my heart knock. Makes me queasy.

I'll leave the snacks and name tags alone.

Others in the circle offer suggestions to Sondra. When the discussion fades, she tosses a small yellow ball she is holding.

Tosses it to me.

I'm amazed that the soft, small, squishy ball smacks into my hands. I'm no athlete.

"Welcome," says Sondra. "You want to go?"

I'm not sure at all.

"Or," says the man in scrubs, "if you want to pass until later, that's fine." I see his name tag now, *James.* "Or you can just tell us your name, and your diagnosis, how long you've had it. Your meds you take. Anything else you do to manage your illness, like therapy, exercise, balanced diet, regular sleep."

I grip the ball. I glance around the circle.

Everybody in there looks like people. If they're dangerous or unbalanced, I can't tell.

And Hal I know.

"I'm Susan," I say. "I have bipolar one disorder. I've been diagnosed nearly four months."

Being able to say those words in this room is freeing.

And by saying them, I've discovered I've just rendered the faces in the circle as belonging to trusted people.

"Welcome, Susan," say several.

"How'd you find us?" says James.

"Hal told me about your meeting." I curve my hand through the air toward Luther's brother.

Hal looks straight at me with a knowledge and a frankness that is hard to ignore. "I think you've done a good thing, Doctor, coming here. A lot in here will tell you, you're in this for the long haul, whether you want to be or not. You might as well have company."

Hal has said what I'm only now beginning to understand.

I can't go back, I can never go back, to the person I used to be.

If I keep on missing that lost part of my life, I will miss the rest of my life.

The one I'm living now.

If I don't go on, how can I return to the college and teach?

Or discover some different way for me.

Or care for myself. And Ian.

Write the book I have to write.

(If I *have* to write the book, is that the same as God giving it to me?

If I have to write, is that a form of *declaring new ways*?

I don't have to answer this right now.)

I look around the circle at these fragile people.

Emphatically, boldly frail before one another.

There is a strange sort of power in that. Declaring membership in the fellowship of the flawed.

I catch Jesus's eye. I take a good look. We are not on speaking terms, I think. I can't say if we ever will be again.

But I can sit there where he can see me, and I'll try not to mind.

TODAY

I have gone on not minding.
Somehow or other, I never stopped.

What has surprised me, amazed me more than all—neither
has he.

We've even been known to talk these days, he and I.

What became of my book, of course, you hold in your hands.

ACKNOWLEDGMENTS

Thanks to the following who graciously offered their assistance and their expertise as I was writing this book: Dr. Anne Mayhew, Professor Emerita, and Dr. Jeanine Williamson, both of the University of Tennessee, Knoxville; attorney Craig Garrett; retired attorney Caesar Stair, formerly partner with Bernstein, Stair, and McAdams; and Dawn and Tina Sullivan. Thanks to the Reverend Laura Rasor and the Reverend Catherine Nance, United Methodist pastors, for the loan of their commentaries.

I consulted a number of print resources while writing this novel. Those of greatest importance include these:

Alter, Robert. *Ancient Israel: The Former Prophets: Joshua, Judges, Samuel and Kings, A Translation with Commentary.* New York: WW Norton and Company, 2013.

Bruggemann, Walter. *First and Second Samuel. Interpretation: A Bible Commentary for Teaching and Preaching.* Atlanta: John Knox Press, 1990.

Willimon, William H. *Acts. Interpretation: A Bible Commentary for Teaching and Preaching.* Atlanta: John Knox Press, 1988.

Particular thanks to the Reverend Laura Rasor for the happy misunderstanding that revealed to me how the story should end.

Thanks to readers Mandy Branch, Wendy Dinwiddie, Erin Fitzgerald, Valerie Gaumont, Jane Hardman, Jane Hicks, Carolyn Hutsell, Linda Hutsell, Carol Luther, Nancy T. McGlasson, Reverend Laura Rasor, Mary Lynn Roy, and Dr. Jeanine Williamson who gave their valuable time, feedback, and support to the project.

I am profoundly grateful to everyone at Paraclete Press for believing in and taking such kind care of this book.

Though years of experience underlie the representations of bipolar disorder in this novel, nothing in the text should be construed as medical or diagnostic advice. If you believe you or someone you know may have symptoms of bipolar disorder, please seek treatment from a qualified medical professional at the earliest opportunity.

Enormous thanks to Jesus for this book in its entirety, beginning to end.

Any mistakes herein are my own.

ABOUT PARACLETE PRESS

Paraclete Press is the publishing arm of the Cape Cod Benedictine community, the Community of Jesus. Presenting a full expression of Christian belief and practice, we reflect the ecumenical charism of the Community and its dedication to sacred music, the fine arts, and the written word.

 The Raven, to ancient peoples, represented light, wisdom, and sustenance, as well as darkness and mystery. In the same spirit, Raven Fiction reflects the whole of human experience, from the darkness of injustice, oppression, doubt, and pain to experiences of awe and wonder, hope, goodness, and beauty.

Learn more about us at our website:
www.paracletepress.com
or phone us toll-free at 1.800.451.5006

SCAN
TO
READ
MORE